W9-ATR-705

DRY COUNTY

DRY C

DUNTY

JAKE HINKSON

PEGASUS CRIME

NEW YORK LONDON

Dry County

Pegasus Crime is an imprint of
Pegasus Books, Ltd.
148 West 37th Street, 13th Floor
New York, NY 10018

Copyright © 2019 by Jake Hinkson

First Pegasus Books hardcover edition October 2019

Interior design by Sabrina Plomitallo-González, Pegasus Books

All rights reserved. No part of this book may be reproduced in whole
or in part without written permission from the publisher, except by reviewers
who may quote brief excerpts in connection with a review in a newspaper, magazine,
or electronic publication; nor may any part of this book be reproduced, stored in a
retrieval system, or transmitted in any form or by any means electronic, mechanical,
photocopying, recording, or other, without written permission from the publisher.

ISBN: 978-1-64313-223-5

10 9 8 7 6 5 4 3 2 1

Printed in the United States of America
Distributed by W. W. Norton & Company

For my friend
Oliver Gallmeister

God owns heaven
but He craves the earth
—Anne Sexton

PART ONE SATURDAY MORNING

ONE RICHARD WEATHERFORD

The cell phone on my nightstand tremors just before daybreak. At first, I fear that something has happened to a member of my congregation. More than once, I've been awakened by the news of a car crash out on the highway, or a family left homeless by a house fire, or someone shaken by the prognosis of cancer. Taking only a moment to rub sleep from my eyes, I steel myself for any of these crises, but when I lift the glowing blue screen to my face and see Gary's number, I almost curse. Slipping out of the sheets, with the phone spasming in my hand, I manage to cross the bedroom without waking my wife.

"Can you talk?" he asks.

My bare feet plod against the cool floors as I rush down the hallway, past the rooms where my children lay sleeping. I take the stairs two at a time. Once I'm safely to the bottom, I turn into the kitchen and whisper, "It's four in the morning."

"It's five," he says. "More like five."

I glance at the digital readout on the microwave. 4:56.

I want to yell at him, but I can't, so my voice comes out in a choked and angry rasp. "I'm in bed with my wife."

"You're talking to me from your bed?"

"No. I got out of bed and came downstairs when my phone vibrated."

Although I'm trying to speak softly, my voice echoes in the large, unoccupied spaces of my home. I have always loved how our enormous kitchen feeds into the dining room, which in turn opens into the living room that runs along the front of the house. Now, however, all this space seems to amplify my whispers into announcements at a ballpark.

I hurry down the hallway to the basement door.

He says, "You were supposed to meet me yesterday."

I ease the door shut behind me. "And you think calling me at home first thing in the morning is the smart thing to do?"

"Did Penny hear the phone go off?"

"Don't say her name."

I clomp down the wooden basement steps and pace the concrete floor between the boys' weight bench and dusty boxes of old knickknacks stacked against the wall.

"Do you hear me?" I say. "Don't say her name."

"Sensitive," he says. "What if I just hang up the phone? Then what happens?"

Steadying myself against a box labeled *Christmas Ornaments* in Penny's immaculate handwriting, I say, "No. Please, don't."

"We need to talk," he says. "Today."

Taking a deep breath, I think, *This is what I get. This is what a fool gets.*

"It would be difficult for me to get away today. It's the busiest time of the year for me. There are things I have to tend to. A lot of things. I can't just leave town."

"Then let's meet in town."

"Gary, no."

"We're just going to talk. And it doesn't have to be a long conversation, either. But it has to happen today. I mean it. I'm not giving you a choice about this."

I find another breath. "Where do you want to meet?"

"Your office."

"I'm not meeting you at the church. Don't be stupid."

"Watch your fucking mouth, Richard."

"I'm not . . . Look, I'm sorry. I'm just saying, think about it. It's the worst place to meet. People will be going in and out of there all day today."

"On a Saturday?"

"Tomorrow's Easter. We have the final preparations for the Passion Play. Musicians, actors, sound and lighting people. The Ladies' Auxiliary will be running in and out of there helping set things up."

"Okay then. Down behind the school."

"You mean that pit back there?"

"Yeah."

"But if someone sees us it will only draw attention to us. You know what I mean?"

"Hey, it's up to you. We can meet in public and try to blend in, or we can meet in secret and try not to get caught. You decide."

I rub my face. "Behind the school, then."

"When can you come?"

"The sooner the better. How about an hour? Can you be there in an hour?"

"Yes."

"Okay."

"Richard?"

"What?"

"If you don't show up today, we're going to move into the consequences phase of things."

I'm standing in my pajama bottoms, in an old T-shirt, with the basement's concrete floor cold against my feet, and I'm frightened beyond measure at the danger posed to me by this boy, but, even so, my voice sounds indignant when I tell him, "I'll be there."

———

I climb the wooden steps, my feet numb and dirty. I go upstairs and try to slip as quietly as I can back into our bedroom.

In my absence, the first faint overtures of the coming sun have lightened the sky outside our windows to a bright, misty gray. Penny turns over to look at me.

"What is it?" she asks.

Reentering the warmth of our bed, I tell her, "Terry Baltimore."

I am amazed how easily this lie comes, not just in its speed but in its perfection. Terry Baltimore is a shattered remnant of a man, all that remains of a life squandered in drunken oblivion. He is one of those men who sporadically appears at any church. He has learned the words to say—he tells me he has given his ruined life to Christ and wants to walk the straight and narrow from here on out—but he still has the stink about him. Not just the stink of booze, but the stink of defeat. I believe that Christ can redeem anyone, but I learned long ago that he will not redeem everyone. For the Terry Baltimores of the world, Christ is just another hustle. I know this, and I endure it because it's my job. My job is not to save Terry Baltimore; my job is to talk the talk of redemption until Terry Baltimore finally decides to move on. They always do. Once they've exhausted the goodwill and disposable charity of some of our older or more gullible church members, the Terry Baltimores always leave without a word, without a trace, never to be heard from again.

"It's five o'clock in the morning," Penny tells me.

"I know. I gather Terry had a long night."

"Ugh."

Again, I'm struck by the perfection of my lie. Penny has a good heart, and her faith is real, but her sense of Christian obligation never strays far from her own comfort. She likes teaching third-grade Sunday school and having luncheons with the ladies because she gets to lead the prayers. She is not one to linger in the grimy, broken world of the Terry Baltimores, faith or no faith. Of all our congregants, Terry is the one she is most likely to believe the worst of and the one she is least likely to speak to about it. He is the perfect excuse.

"Well," she says, "what did he want?"

"He wants to see me, wants to pray with me. I take it he's having a crisis of faith."

"When?"

"Now."

"Now? It's—"

"I know what time it is, dear."

"On the Saturday before Easter, of all days."

"I pointed that out to him."

"I bet you didn't. What does he want to pray about?"

I shrug.

She asks, "And you're going to go?"

I turn to her. It's funny, but I'm actually disappointed in her lack of charity. "Don't you think I should? In your heart of hearts, do you think the Lord wants me to lie here in bed while a man who has called me for help languishes on the other side of town?"

She hugs her body pillow and closes her eyes.

I tell her, "I'll run over there and . . . do whatever. Then I'll be back. An hour, tops."

"Okay," she says. "Just try not to wake up your children, please. The little ones are going to come jumping on me the second their eyes open."

I kiss her forehead and walk to the bathroom. I would like to throw on some clothes and go now, but I should do this as normally as possible. I should get ready and conduct myself as if nothing's out of the ordinary, and that means adhering to my usual morning regimen.

Running the shower until it's hot, I undress and get in. The scalding water lashes my skin, shocking any remaining sluggishness out of me. I lather up. I clean my body, but when I shut off the water and step from the shower, my steaming skin still dripping, a groan escapes my throat, involuntarily.

God, I am so sorry.

Please help me.

Please make him leave.

I wrap a towel around my waist and shave my face over the sink. My hair is plastered to my scalp, accentuating my large features. I'm handsome, in a makeshift kind of way. Photographed at a good angle—as I was for the staff picture on our church website—I am a good-looking man. Caught at the wrong angle, however, my attractiveness looks as if it were assembled from spare parts. My ears stick out a bit, my nose is disproportionate to my cheeks, and my lips slightly overwhelm my jaw.

That's the way it looks to me this morning, less like a face that God made and more like some kind of genetic accident.

I shake my head. The mirror is the quickest route away from God.

By the time I leave to go meet Gary, sunlight is creeping through the trees at the edge of my yard and the neighborhood is yawning and stretching itself awake. I back the Odyssey out of the driveway and wave at Mr. Newman, who is retrieving his paper from the lawn next door.

He waves at me, then points to the sign in his yard that reads: KEEP VAN BUREN COUNTY DRY.

I have the same sign, of course. We give each other a thumbs-up.

Down the street, Carrie Close is loading her children into her hatchback. Her boy Allen has his swimming lessons down in Little Rock on Saturdays, and she has to leave early to get there on time. Carrie seems to be speaking harshly to Allen and his younger sisters as she shuts the rear door, but when she sees me, she smiles and waves.

At the end of the road, I turn onto School Hill Road. Climbing the hill, I pass a large red truck blasting music. The music is country, I suppose, though twenty-five years ago, when I was in high school, it would have been considered rock. Either way, it's turned up too loud for an early Saturday morning.

School Hill Road swings past the high school. Down the hill, past the middle and elementary school buildings, the blacktop disintegrates into a gravel road that runs by the rodeo arena—a large dirt pen flanked by unpainted bleachers, with an announcer's box in the middle. Past that, before the road reaches the baseball field, I turn right across an empty green field toward the trees.

I didn't grow up in Stock, so I didn't learn the town's nooks and crannies as a child. Since I was called to pastor this church ten years ago, however,

Penny and I have raised our children here. Although the older ones, all college age, were born when we lived in North Carolina, they came of age in Arkansas. The little ones were born here and have never known anything else. As a result, my children are natives of this place, while, in some ways, I think I'll always feel like an immigrant freshly arrived on its strange shores. The kids have taught me its language, showed me its customs. They've also taught me certain things through the gossip they've brought home. And one thing I know about is the hidden pit near the trees between the rodeo ring and the baseball diamond.

The field looks normal from the gravel road, just a grassy slope gently rising toward the tree line. If you turn off the road and drive toward the trees, however, you discover that after rising for a bit the ground suddenly plunges into a large pit that's invisible to the road. This, I am told, is where the bad kids go to drink.

I pull up to the edge of the worn earthen crater. At its charred center, a bonfire's remains look like the impact site of a bomb. I get out of the mini-van and tromp down the loose dirt to this scarred, blackened soil. Old beer cans. A broken bottle. Cigarette butts.

"Good morning, Brother Weatherford," Gary says, walking out of the trees, his hands in the pockets of his dark jeans.

I scan the top of the pit.

"There's no one around," he says. He slides down the crumbling crater wall and stops on the other side of the ashes. "Kids don't come out here this early, so neither do the cops."

His narrow face is pale, and he's wearing a dark windbreaker over a black T-shirt with some secular band on it. He's a college dropout, but in the diffuse morning light, he almost looks too young to have been to university. The sight of him slightly nauseates me.

"You know you can't call me," I tell him. "What were you thinking?"

"I was thinking about how I drove all the way to Petit Jean and sat there for an hour waiting for you."

"I told you I was busy. My kids are all in town for Easter."

"Don't hide behind your children," he says. "It's so gross."

My face flushes. "I'm here now."

"Then let's get to it. Where's my money?"

"*Your* money? You mean *my* money."

"Which you said you would give to me."

"I said I'd think about it."

"Why are you doing this to me, Richard?"

"What am I doing to you?"

"You're forcing me to hurt you. I don't want to do that. That's not who I am."

"Really? You're not blackmailing me?"

He stares at me with the kind of disappointment that I sometimes use against my children. No one else in my life, not even Penny, ever regards me with such open condescension. I hate myself for giving him that kind of power.

He says, "We agreed together that the best thing for me was to move on, to get out of this shithole and start over somewhere else. Hell, it was your idea."

"All I said was—"

He dismisses my defense with a wave of his hand. "I only want what you promised me. If you want to stand here and debate, we can do that, but every second we do we run the risk of someone seeing us together."

I look up at the top of the pit, bare dirt against a limestone blue sky.

Gary says, "See? That's what this is all about. You don't want to be seen with me. Ever. You don't want people to know about us. Ever. You got what you wanted from me, and now you want me to just disappear. But that can't happen until you give me thirty thousand dollars. You understand that? I'm not blackmailing you. You're paying me to move away and act like I don't know you. It's about what *you* want *me* to do. I'm just not going to do it for free."

I rub my eyes. "Where am I supposed to get thirty thousand dollars?"

"You're the one always telling me how successful you are. You can get that much."

"Not like that, not with no one knowing. I don't just have thirty grand stuck in a drawer somewhere."

"Well, you need to find it somewhere," he says calmly, like he's telling a child to clean their room. "I'm done waiting." He turns his attention back to the mound of cold ashes and charred beer cans. "If you don't help me out, then I guess I'll just stay in town and tell the truth."

"You really want to be the local scandal?"

With a smile, he shakes his head and kicks some dirt into the ashes. "These rednecks have been calling me a faggot since the fifth grade, Richard. They'll just say, 'We knew it.' You're the one with the good reputation hanging around his neck like a noose."

Trying to sound confident, I try the only thing I have left. I tell him, "It would be my word against yours. People would believe me."

"Some would, sure. But honestly, how many people would have to believe me before it ruined your reputation with everyone? Ten? Five? One?" Gary nudges a broken bottle with the toe of his boot. "Really, all it would take is Penny."

I want to step through the ashes and grab him, ball up his shirt in my fist, and hit him as hard as I can. But I can't move.

"What did you say to me?" is all I can get out.

He turns his face to me now, his expression almost pitying. As if he's being the most reasonable man in the world, he says, "It's all up to you, Richard. If you give me the money to leave, I'll leave. I'll just go away. And then your life can be normal again. Isn't that what you want?"

My head swims, and I have to close my eyes to keep from losing my balance. "I'll kill you if you go near my family . . . ," I say.

The threat doesn't faze him at all. He just says, "It would be a lot easier to help me leave town."

When I open my eyes, they're wet. My mouth is dry. There's a ringing in my ears. It's as if he has slapped me.

Blood-pink splotches mottle his pale face, and his slender chest rises against his shirt, but his eyes are as empty as a school shooter's.

He's not just a boy. He can really do this. He knows what to say, and he knows who to say it to.

"All right, goddamn you," I say, taking the Lord's name in vain for the first time in years. "I'll get you your money."

TWO BRIAN HARTEN

The motherfucking car alarm wakes me up. I've always hated that thing. Roxie had it put in as a birthday present one year. "Who's gonna steal my car in Stock?" I asked her. She said I was an ungrateful asshole.

Fair enough. Now she's gone, but I've still got the alarm.

Good thing this morning, I guess. The alarm is blaring away while I haul my ass out of bed—in nothing but boxers—and pull up the blinds.

Two guys in the parking lot of the apartment complex are loading my car onto a big white tow truck. One of them turns off my car alarm somehow. I'm not sure how he does that, but it just stops.

I run to the door and throw it open. "Hey!" I yell at the guy standing by the controls to the lift.

He's as big as the truck. Got a big bald head white as the sun. He kinda gives me a side-eye glance but keeps working the levers.

The other guy comes around the side of the truck. He's ratty, with a tiny mouth and fucked-up front teeth that pinch together like an ax-head.

He says, "Repossessed, man."

"Fuck that. Put my car down."

He holds up a piece of paper. "You Brian Harten?"

"Yeah."

"This your car?"

"Yeah."

"Been repossessed, man."

I take the paper from him and wipe my ass with it and throw it on the ground.

"What do you think of that?" I say.

"C'mon, man, I ain't even had breakfast yet," the little rat says.

The big guy tells him, "I said you shoulda got something with me at McDonald's."

The little rat turns to him. "I done told you, man, I'm off the animals. For good."

"Shoulda got a egg and cheese biscuit, then."

"Animals *and* animal products, man. I'm off them."

"You can't be a vegan in this town," the big guy says.

"Bullshit I can't."

"What are you gonna do, live on nuts and berries and shit?"

"Put my fucking car down!" I yell. I step toward the little guy.

"Whoa, Dude-in-His-Boxers," he says, "just back up. You want to yell at someone, get on the phone and yell at your creditors. We can't help you." He turns to the big guy. "And you, man—you don't even know what you're talking about. You read that book I give you?"

"I ain't reading a fucking book, man. I didn't read books when they *made* us read books. And if I *was* gonna read a book, it wouldn't be a book about fucking vegans and shit."

"The animals, man."

"Fuck the animals, man."

"I can pay you guys," I say. "Twenty bucks each. Just tell them you couldn't find me."

"Can't do it, buddy."

"Thirty bucks each."

"Nope. Sorry. You should go call whoever you gotta call. We gotta take the car."

I jab a finger into the rat's scrawny shoulder. "You're not listening to me, asshole. I need that car."

He turns to me and puts his little face in mine, his nasty teeth sticking out from under his top lip. "Don't touch me again. Ain't gonna be a second warning."

I step back and swing on him. I don't know why. Fucking dumb. I'm out here, one pair of boxer shorts between my bare dick and the whole world, and I swing on him.

I get him in the face, but it hurts my hand more than it hurts him, and then he turns into Jason Bourne all the sudden. Hits me three times before I can blink, then sweeps my legs and drops me to the pavement. Gives me one more punch in the face to get the point across.

I cover up. He backs off and calls me a shithead.

The big guy is laughing his ass off.

They load into the truck. The little guy is rubbing his knuckles and cussing me, and the big guy is saying, "Kung Tofu, my man!"

They drive off, and I watch my car disappear down the street.

I get up. Put a hand to my nose. My face feels like it's blowing up like a balloon. Blood drips down on my hairy white belly. My leg is scraped where I hit the pavement.

"Fuck."

I turn around to limp back inside, and every neighbor I have is peeking out their blinds. I flip off all of them and go to my door.

Locked.

I cuss that door like it fucked my wife.

God. Damn. It. All.

I hobble around to the back of the apartments. My patio gate is locked, so I stand on the air-conditioning unit and pull myself over, scrapping my leg in the process.

Please, Jesus. Let the sliding glass door—

It's locked.

Cocksucker. Cock-fucking-sucker.

I unlock the patio gate and walk around to Erikson's apartment and knock.

He comes to the door, and I can smell weed and bacon behind him. He's dressed like he's going somewhere, but he never leaves the apartments, so I guess he's just up and at 'em early this morning.

"Seen what happened," he says.

"Yeah, listen—"

"Got your ass kicked."

"Yeah."

"That ol' boy was small, but he sure had some moves on him."

"I'm locked out of my apartment."

He looks me up and down and nods. He's got the apartment keys on his belt. "Let's go," he says.

As I follow him to my door, he says, "Repossessed your ride, huh?"

"I reckon."

"That mean you're gonna have trouble making rent?"

"No."

He shoots me a look over his shoulder.

"Hey, man," I tell him, "I pay you when the rent is due. 'Til then, you ain't got any right to hassle me about it."

We get to my door, and he unlocks it. "Front-door service," he says.

"Yeah. Thanks."

He looks at the blood smeared across my gut. "That little feller sure whooped your ass."

I go inside and hop in the shower. They took my fucking car. I stick my head under the water.

Now what?

Ray. I need to go see Ray. He can loan me the cash.

After I check my face to make sure my nose ain't broke, I get dressed and rush out the door.

As I cut through the town square, past the courthouse and Pickett's, my nose still hurts. I keep touching it, afraid it's going to start bleeding again. But it's fine. Just hurts.

Stock.

I hate this town.

No, that ain't true. I don't hate it. I like it just fine. I just wish the assholes who run things around here would give me a break.

I get to the sidewalk that runs up School Hill Road and start climbing it. Fucker is steep. I ain't walked it since I was a kid. Used to go down to Pickett's to play Pac-Man in the foyer. Got busted shoplifting a Coke there once. Stupid thing to do. Lady let me go, though. She was pretty nice.

I pass through a little neighborhood. Nice houses, with signs in the yards that either read, TRUMP: MAKE AMERICA GREAT AGAIN or TED CRUZ 2016. Don't see any Hillary or Bernie signs—not in this neighborhood, anyway— but just about every yard has a sign that reads, KEEP VAN BUREN COUNTY DRY.

Assholes. What happened to freedom in America, man? These people don't give a shit about drinking. Not really. Half the people in this town have beer sitting in their fridge right now. These "Keep the County Dry" assholes just want to tell other people what to do. They don't care who they hurt. It's taken me six months just to get the quorum court to agree to have a vote on whether to put the measure on a special ballot.

Fucking local preachers fought me every step. Weatherford, that asshole from First Baptist, he's the main one. It's pathetic. *Pathetic.* You're telling me that your whole damn mission in life is to make sure other people can't buy a drink in town? Jesus turned water into wine, didn't he? I brought that up at the last city council meeting. Weatherford said the wine was really just unfermented grape juice. Now how the fuck can he know that? JC's wine was pinot fucking noir, for all Richard Weatherford knows.

Top of the hill, I turn onto Ray's road. He's got a small house, a front yard, one tree. I could live in a place like this if we get the store up and going. Nothing fancy, not at first. That's how people screw up. Like all the rock stars and rappers and stuff. They get some money, and then they blow it all like idiots. Not me. I'm just gonna get me a little house with a yard to start out.

I knock on his door.

Takes a minute, but Ray opens up and looks surprised. "Hey, man . . ."

"They repossessed my car, dude."

"What?"

"Guys came by this a.m. and hauled it off."

"Shit."

He walks outside, which is kind of funny. Usually we just go inside. Don't think we've ever walked around his yard before, but that's what he does. Hands in the back pockets of his jeans, hair shoved under a bandana, he looks around his property like he's never seen it before.

"You think you could spot me the cash to get it back?" I ask. "I need some wheels to run around and do the shit we need to do before the vote. I'll pay you back once the cash gets freed up."

He takes a breath. "Yeah, listen, Brian, I've been thinking. Me and Lacy been talking. I think maybe . . . I think maybe the store ain't gonna happen."

I just stare at him for a minute before I can think to say, "What are you talking about?"

He lifts his hand and kinda gestures at everything all at once. "Dude, this town ain't ready for a liquor store. We were talking last night, and Lacy made the point, she said, 'You know, maybe in ten years, maybe in five, the town will be ready. But not now.' I think that's true. Just think about how everybody has lost their shit over this thing. I mean, they already made all these 'Keep the County Dry' signs, and that was just to stop the special ballot from happening. And now they're talking like we might have to wait until the general election in November to put it in the ballot? *November*, man. They could keep putting this off forever. We moved too quick on this thing. Should have took it slower."

I walk toward him. "Dude, what are you doing?"

"What? Nothing. I'm just—"

"Ray, don't do this, man. All the money I got is tied up in this store. Hell, all the money I *don't* got is tied up in this store. They fucking hauled off my car, man. I got *nothing*. You know what I'm saying? If we don't get this store opened, I got *nothing*."

He can't even look at me. Stares at the ground like a pussy. "I'm sorry, Brian. I'm sorry as hell. If this thing would've come together the way we thought it was going to, we'd be in there already. And I loved the idea of having a place. You know I did."

"*Did?* Dude, don't talk like it's already over."

He takes a deep breath. "This is the hardest thing I've ever done, Brian, but I'm gonna need to back out."

"Is this Lacy talking? Get her out here." I start toward the house. "Let me talk to her."

"She ain't here, man."

"Where is she?"

"Work."

"Let's go inside and talk about this."

"I can't. The kids are asleep."

I jab my thumb at my heart. "I got kids, too, Ray. I got kids, too. What about my kids?"

He lowers his head like he's just trying to wait out the storm, like I'm his alcoholic father or something. I can tell he doesn't want to talk. He doesn't have anything left to say. All he wants is for me to leave so he can go back inside.

"Ray . . ."

"I'm sorry, Brian. I'm sorry as hell. I know how much this means to you."

"What are you going to do, man? Just keep working at the cement place?"

"Yeah."

"You hate it."

"No, I don't," he says. "I liked the idea of opening a store with you, sure. But I don't hate my job. I'm gonna go to work on Monday like always, and I'll be fine."

"Yeah, well, I won't. I told Tommy to go fuck himself, so I don't have a job anymore."

He shakes his head. "God. I'm sorry, man."

"I thought I had a partner I could count on. That's why I quit my job."

"No." His face gets hot, and he points at me. "*You* did that. Not me. Don't put that on me. I didn't tell my boss to go fuck himself. If you went off half-cocked on Tommy Weller, that's on you."

"You're a fucking pussy, man. A pussy-whipped little . . . pussy who don't know what being a man is all about."

"What's it about, Brian? You tell me."

"It's about following your dreams. It's about believing in yourself."

"You're calling *me* a pussy? You sound like Céline Dion."

I throw up my hands. "Forget it, man. Just please don't do this. Just wait until the vote."

"We back out now, we cut our losses, we can still get out of this thing without losing our asses."

"Not me," I say. "I *need* this store to open. I *need* it to open, Ray. I moved back here. I'm the one who put up the money for O'Keefe to hold the property for us."

"Hey, man, I put up my share."

"I know. I know. I'm just saying, I can't take this hit. You got a job—two jobs with Lacy's. I quit my job. I can't take this hit, man. I'll lose my ass. I'll have to declare fucking bankruptcy."

He hangs his head like it weighs a million pounds. He says, "I'm so sorry, Brian. I really am." And the thing is, I know he's sorry. He looks like he could start crying. But he doesn't. Instead, he takes the heaviest breath I ever saw a man take, and he says, "I know you're disappointed in me. We just moved too fast on this deal. Simple as that. Rookie mistake. We should have concentrated on getting the vote passed first. That's as much my fault as yours. I really thought we had it all locked up, too, but we didn't. We were fucked the first time the quorum court refused to vote on it. We started losing money right then and there. And we got to face that. If we get out now, we'll only lose what we already paid O'Keefe. That's a hard loss, but it's better than pumping more money and time into a place that ain't never going to open. Not in this town. Not now. And that's the bottom line. It's just not going to happen, man. I'm sorry, but it's just not going to happen."

I want to say something to him. Call him a pussy again, cuss him out, beg him, but I've already shot my wad. I got nothing left. He goes to his door, opens it, and walks inside. He never looks back at me.

THREE SARABETH SIMMONS

Nicki Minaj blasts me out of my sleep. "No Frauds," way too early, way too loud.

I reach for my phone. Shit. Pickett's.

"I'm on my way," I say.

"You're late," that fucking bitch tells me.

"I know," I say, swinging my feet to the floor. "I'm on my way. I had car trouble."

"You're late," she says again. It's all she's got to say.

I hang up.

I sit there on my bed for a second with my head in my hands. There's a stabbing pain behind my right eye, and the whole inside of my head feels like it's trying to get out. My stomach feels like it's trying to get out, too, but I'm not going to puke. I'm not a puker.

I get up and walk to the bedroom door. I listen a second to see if Tommy is still here. He's going to work today, I think. I don't hear anything, so I open the door and stick my head out. Nothing.

I hurry to the bathroom and lock the door. I'm kind of shocked when I see my reflection in the mirror.

Maybe it's just that I'm hungover, but I can't believe that this is my face, my body. Gary says I'm beautiful, but Gary's a sweetheart. My head is shaped like a box, but my chin is pointy. My eyes are too big, and my mouth is too small. My belly is bigger than my tits, and my ass is basically nonexistent.

Ugh.

I pee, and while I'm sitting there, I put my face in my hands. My weird-shaped head hates me this morning.

I need to stop drinking. I just turned nineteen years old, and I been drinking like I'm in a fucking country song since I was fifteen. It's stupid.

I wash up. I don't have time to take a shower, but I brush my teeth and put on deodorant. Then I pull on my cleanest jeans, dig a shirt out of the closet, grab my work vest, and head out the door.

I'm all the way down the hall before I realize Tommy and Momma are in the kitchen.

He's just wearing boxers and socks, and his big gut is whiter than an uncooked turkey. Momma says he wears socks in bed, which I think might be the worst damn thing I ever heard. He's sitting at the table polishing his old high school baseball trophies with a piece of suede while Momma cooks him breakfast. She's wearing his shirt and a pair of pink panties. Just what I want to see first thing in the morning.

"Well, look who's up bright and early," Tommy says. He puts down the trophy. His hair is sticking out in all directions, and he's sitting there in his underwear and dirty socks, but he's got a look on his face like he's about to conduct a job interview.

"Up late," I say. "Gotta get to work."

I sit down at the kitchen table and start putting on my socks and shoes.

"What time you supposed to be there?" he asks.

I shrug.

"*This*"—he mocks my shrug—"ain't no time."

Momma is making French toast. She doesn't turn around, just keeps whisking eggs.

Tommy says, "So what time were you supposed to be at work?"

I'm tying my shoe. "I don't have to tell you what time. I'm gonna get yelled at when I get there. Don't need you yelling at me here."

"You need somebody yelling at you here, I guess," he says. "Ain't supposed to go rolling in to work an hour late."

I pull on my other shoe.

He says, "What would it be if everybody come in an hour late?"

I stop what I'm doing and stare at him. "I wish they would. Then people would stop giving me shit." I go back to my shoes. "Besides, it ain't any of your business what I do or when I do it."

He turns to Momma's back. "I don't know what you were thinking raising a daughter to be like this one here. No man wants to be around *this* first thing in the morning."

Momma puts some bread in the pan and moves it around with a fork.

Tommy looks back at me. "You could learn a thing or two from me, girl. You ever stop to consider that I'm the most successful motherfucker you know?"

"That's a depressing thought." I tie my other shoe.

He says, "I own four businesses."

"I've heard."

"Long as I'm paying the rent here—"

"You ain't renting me," I say.

"Long as I'm paying the rent around here—"

"And I get you a discount on groceries at Pickett's."

I stand up.

He stands up, too. "Long as I'm paying the rent around here," he says, "I'll say whatever the fuck I want to say."

He just stands there like he's making some big point.

I tell him, "Long as you're standing up, why don't you go put on some clothes."

He smiles and looks at Momma's back. She's stacking the French toast on a plate. He turns back to me and pulls down the front of his boxers and shows me his hairy junk.

"Gross!" I yell. "Momma . . . !"

Tommy sits down. Momma pours herself a cup of coffee. She turns her head just enough to say over her shoulder, "Sarabeth, you ain't getting any less late to work."

I pull into the employee parking next to the dumpsters behind Pickett's. I take a deep breath before I get out of the car. It's five after nine, so I'm over an hour late.

As I walk past the dumpsters, the smell of rotting produce hits me like a hammer. My head's still throbbing, and my eyes still hurt. Now my heart starts thumping. I open the back door and go inside. *Why am I scared?* The stock room is empty, and the lights are off in the manager's office. I clock in and walk up to the salesfloor.

I groan a little when I see we have no customers. At least if we had some shoppers, I could avoid that bitch. But she's the only one in the whole store. She's up front on the register.

When she hears me walk in, she turns around and crosses her arms and stares at me. She's tall, with two chins and a hairdo that she sprayed into place back in 1994. I walk up and stand on the opposite side of the register.

I just stare back at her for a while until it gets uncomfortable. Then I look away and glance around the store. It's bright and clean. All the lights are on. Everything is in its place. Just another quiet Saturday morning. One person can run the store until damn near noon. Most people in town just drive over to Walmart, anyway. This bitch knows it, and so do I.

"Do you have anything to say?" she finally asks.

I turn back to her. "I had car trouble."

"That's it? You come in an hour and a half late, and that's all you have to say?"

"I'm an hour late."

"You're supposed to be here half an hour before we open; you know that."

I sigh. "I'm sorry I had car trouble."

"What kind of car trouble did you have?"

My face gets hot. What am I, a fucking mechanic? And why the interrogation?

"I don't know. It wouldn't start."

"How'd you get here?"

"It finally started."

She stares at me. Sure, I'm lying, but what's it to her? She hasn't done anything for the last hour. Stood here. Posted boring shit on Facebook. Maybe sold a newspaper or a gallon of milk. If I'd been here, I just would have been standing around while she sat in the back telling Facebook about her breakfast.

"I need you here to watch the front," she says. "I have work to do in the back."

Yeah, the world's dullest Facebook account ain't going to update itself.

"Okay."

She logs herself off the register. I log myself on.

"We're not done talking about this," she says.

I nod, and she walks to the back, shaking her head.

I stand behind the register and dig my cell phone out of my pocket. I go to Facebook and go to her profile.

Five.

Four.

Three.

Two.

One.

She updates her status:

A word of Advice to the Youth of America. Be at the place where your supposed to be when your supposed to be there!!! Okay??? It will help you keep your job!!!

Just to be a bitch, I hit Like on her status and put my phone back in my pocket.

An old man walks by the front of the store and waves. I wave back. He keeps walking. I notice he's carrying a Walmart bag.

A little before lunch, Gary texts me, You at work?

Yeah, I write back.

Im going to come see you.

Better not, I tell him.

??

That bitch, I text back. I was late and shes acting like a real whore about it

A minute or two goes by, and then he texts, I talked to Holy Shit.

I almost yelp. When?

This morning

Where?

At the pit

Did he g

"Are you texting?"

I jump and look up, and that bitch is basically right beside me.

"You startled me," I tell her.

She just stares at me with her stupid face.

She's about to say something when Jason comes in. He's already got on his vest. "Morning," he says.

"Jason," she tells him, "after you get clocked in, come right on up here."

He says okay and goes to the back.

"When he gets up here," she says, "you come see me."

She passes Jason on his way back to the registers, and I hear her tell him, "Go ahead and log in on register one."

When he walks up, he asks me, "How's it going?"

"I was a *little* late this morning," I tell him, "and now she's acting like I've been out campaigning for Hillary."

Jason smiles and shakes his head.

I log out. He logs in. I head to the back.

She's sitting at her desk pretending to be looking at some forms.

I stick my head in the doorway. "Hey."

She turns in her chair. "You might want to sit down."

I cross over and sit down. "Okay."

"We're going to have to let you go."

"'Cause I'm late."

"I mean, you really want me to go into all the ways you've earned getting fired? You were late. Again. Not the first time. Not the fifth time. Now you're up there texting."

"There's no one in the store."

She nods. "Yeah. I knew you were going to say that."

"Because it's true."

She smiles. She's got the answer ready, and she's in such a rush to get it out, her voice cracks. "*Pickett's* doesn't pay you to text."

"Does it pay you to post shit on Facebook?"

Now she gets an ugly look on her face. "Sarabeth, I don't need to hear any more of that kind of language. You can just go ahead and punch out and go on home."

"Maybe we should talk to Mr. Pickett."

She spreads her palms. "I already talked to Mr. Pickett, dear, but you are more than welcome to call him." She pushes her phone across the desk. "Here. I'll even dial his number for you."

She ain't bluffing, either. It ain't like Pickett knows me or gives a shit about me. He'd chew me out and tell me I had it coming while she sat there and watched.

I just stand up and walk out. Behind me, I hear her get up and follow me down the hall to the clock.

I turn around. "What are you doing?"

"I'm escorting you out. That's the way it's done."

"You think I'm going to steal something?"

"C'mon, Sarabeth, let's just get you out of here."

She watches as I punch out, and then she follows me to the back door.

I swing the door hard, trying to slam it shut, but it has one of those little bike-pump-looking things at the top that cushions the door and makes it impossible to slam. I hear it click shut behind me.

I stomp over to my car and fire it up. I tear out of the parking lot.

It don't take long, though, before I realize I don't know where I'm going.

I just drive around town. My mind is weirdly clear now, like I just came out of my hangover. Heading away from downtown and the square, I get on the highway and pass by the gas stations and the McDonald's and the Dollar General and the Subway. They all seem small and plastic to me right now. Why is that? Through the windows, I see the people standing in line, or walking out to their cars, and none of them seem any more real to me than the plastic signs. I drive past the big Cowboy Supply and Feed store— two shitkickers in Stetsons are leaning against their trucks talking—and then I'm crossing over the Little Red River Bridge. It's high over the water. When I first got my driver's license, I used to have dreams that I would drive across this bridge and the end would disappear and I'd zoom right off like a ramp. Far down the river, I can barely make out the tiny figure of a man in a boat fishing in the shade.

The highway curves, and on the left, down a little slope, is Stock First Baptist Church.

I dig out my cell, scroll to Gary's name, and press Call.

"Hey," he says.

"I got fired."

"What? When?"

"Now. Just now. That fucking cunt drug me into her office and fired me."

I can hear him breathing as he thinks about that. I pass the KFC, the horse vet, the library. "Well," he says, "fuck her. And that place. Because the good news is you don't need that job anymore."

My heart almost explodes. "You got the money?"

"Not yet. But he said he'll get it."

"Oh."

"Yeah. First thing this morning I called him and woke him up. Got his ass out of bed to come meet me."

"He tell you why he didn't show up at Petit Jean?"

"With his kids, he said. Couldn't get away."

"What about the money?"

"Said he'd get it."

"But you told him he *has* to give you the money, right?"

"Yes."

"That's the only way this will work—if you tell him he doesn't have a choice."

"I know. I told him I'd tell his wife."

"Hell yeah. And everybody else in town."

"Sure, but she's the one he's afraid of. Hell hath no fury like a woman scorned."

"Is that from the Bible?"

"William Congreve. From a play I read in college."

"You're so fucking smart, Gary."

"A play I read in college *before I flunked out . . .*"

I laugh.

I get to the stoplight up by the post office, take a right, and pull into the Walmart parking lot. There are a bunch of cars, but they're all clustered near the front. I park at the very end of the lot and just sit there.

"So, what do you think he'll do?" I ask.

"He'll find a way to get the money."

"And you're sure of that?"

"Yes. You should have seen him when I said I was going to go to his wife. I thought he was going to shit himself."

"Because hell has no fury like a pissed-off preacher's wife."

"That's right."

"But what if . . . Just for the sake of argument, say she doesn't care. Then what?"

"Amos Pettibone."

"What?"

"I go to Amos Pettibone."

"Who the fuck is Amos Pettibone?"

"The chairman of the deacons."

"I don't know what that means."

"Well, if the preacher is the CEO of the church, then the deacons are like the board of directors. They're the ones who could actually fire him. And Richard and Amos hate each other the way only two Christians can. They shake hands and smile and say, 'Brother, the Lord gave me a message to give to you,' and then they very sweetly tell the other guy to go fuck himself. When Richard and I first started messing around, he used to make me swear to never tell anyone. He was always super paranoid about it. All that 'This is our little secret' shit, you know? It was Brother Amos. Brother Amos is the one he's scared of. The wife and the deacon. It's a one-two punch."

"Good," I say. I let out a sigh. "That sounds good. I'm just so damn ready to get out of here. I can't keep living with Momma and Tommy or I'm gonna slit my wrist."

"Well, don't buy a razor just yet," Gary says. "Richard's got to pay us. What else can he do?"

FOUR RICHARD WEATHERFORD

By the time I make it home, the children are awake. The older kids are all doing their own thing. Mary is helping her mother prepare breakfast while Matthew reads the newspaper at the kitchen table. Mark is in the bathroom upstairs. Because of his challenges, it takes him a little longer than the others to do things. As he's getting ready, I hear his slurred voice warbling along atonally to an Elvis gospel song.

In the living room, the two little ones are arguing about something. I've barely closed the front door before Johnny and Ruth rush up and demand that I arbitrate their petty dispute.

"I don't . . . Not now, kids."

Johnny says, "But, Dad—"

I grab his small chin and bend down to lock eyes with him. All my children know what this means. "Not now, Jonathan."

"Yes, sir," he quivers. As I start toward the kitchen, I can hear his little sister, suddenly overcome with either guilt or compassion, tell him that they can both share whatever silly object they were fighting over. Without trying—in fact, by actively avoiding the argument altogether—I've resolved their quarrel.

Penny turns to me from the kitchen sink. The sleeves of her charcoal jumper are pushed up to her elbows, and she's washing orange rinds and eggshells down the garbage disposal. She asks, "Well, how'd it go?"

"What?"

Matthew puts down the paper. "How was Terry Baltimore? I wish you would have gotten me up. I would have liked to have gone with you." Of my children, Matthew is the only one I've ever taken with me on visitations.

"Visiting with Terry would be a trial by fire," Mary tells him. She's pretty, my Mary, with strawberry-blonde hair like her mother. She's cut it quite short, though, and I don't much care for it. I thought I might say something about it, but Penny cautioned me against it. *She already knows you don't like it*, she said. *How?* I asked. *Because you've mentioned it twice already since she's been home*, she said. *But I didn't say anything bad about it. I merely noted how short it was.* Penny said, *You noting it twice is like anyone else saying something bad about it.* I don't always defer to Penny's wisdom about our children—mothers are somewhat overpraised for their intuition, I think—but I trust she knows more about Mary's hair than I do.

"So," Penny says, "how did it go?"

I raise my hands in a mock gesture of futility. For a brief and terrible moment, I realize that everyone is awaiting my reply, preemptive smiles queued on their lips because they know I'll say something funny about Terry Baltimore. The terrible part of it is how counterfeit I feel at the sudden realization that I am about to tell all of these people I love a lie.

I sigh. "He's Terry Baltimore."

They all chuckle, a little let down, perhaps, because I didn't say something about how Terry Baltimore is a trial put here by the Lord or how I'm still praying for a miracle. They all go back to what they were doing.

Penny watches me as I begin to move toward the door. She asks, "Are you going to call your father? We're nearly ready to eat."

I almost groan. I forgot about the phone call to my father. It's an important tradition between us. My mother was always the interpersonal conduit of our family, so all information and affection between my father and myself passed through her. When she died, the year I turned thirty, my father and I lost our emotional translator. As a result, we have each retreated into our own lives. I have my family and my church. My father has his neighbors and a couple of old buddies from the Corps. The only exceptions to this shared silence are Easter and Christmas, when one of us calls the other and we go through the motions of catching up. Like bad Christians, we only show up on holidays, these phone calls our only rituals.

"I'm going to go to my office to do the prayer list. I'll call him later."

I walk down the hall to my office and find Johnny sitting on the floor, his arms wrapped around his legs, brooding.

"Johnny, I need the office."

He doesn't respond, which is a pet peeve of mine.

"Did you hear me?"

"Yes, sir."

He climbs to his feet and makes quite a show of slinking dejectedly out of the room. Clearly, the boy wants my attention, perhaps wanting to relitigate the earlier dispute with Ruth.

I don't have the time for such nonsense, though. I close the door behind him. I don't have a lock on the door, nor do I need one. Everyone in the family knows not to come in when the door is closed. They know to knock only in case something requires my urgent attention. When the door is closed, it's understood that I'm in consultation with the Lord.

I descend to my knees and clasp my hands.

Please, God . . .

I've prayed for thousands of people in my life, maybe tens of thousands. People in need. People in pain. The sick. The dying. The saved and the unsaved. But now I try to pray for myself, and it's as if I've never prayed before. I don't know how to speak to God. Not about this. Of course, he already knows. He's seen everything I've done. Which is exactly why I can't talk to him about it, why I can ask for neither forgiveness nor help.

I broke this, and now I have to fix this.

If I don't give this boy money, he'll ruin me. That is the crisis I'm in.

Would Penny forgive me? What if I told her before Gary could?

My answer is a wave of nausea.

I think of a night with Penny more than a year ago, months before I began to see Gary. Our physical coldness—*my* physical coldness—led to a fight late one night, to tears and hard words whispered so the children wouldn't hear. *Do we really have to talk about this?* I asked. *You haven't touched me since I had Ruth,* she said. *Do you know how that makes me feel? Look,* I said, *men just get older. I've already given you five children.* Penny shook her head. *I'm not talking about making children, Richard. I need to know that I'm still attractive. I'm not some old woman. Am I supposed to go another forty years without sex? Am I supposed to go another forty years without feeling like someone wants me?*

I don't know why I couldn't simply give her the reassurances she wanted that night. I think I was afraid that she'd want me to prove my attraction to her. Instead, I became indignant, accusing her of thinking about sex in a worldly way. The next day, she apologized to me. She swallowed her own humiliation because she felt she'd hurt me, insulted my masculine pride. We haven't returned to the subject—or touched each other—since.

I can't even really contemplate telling her about Gary. It's like contemplating suicide. And if this became public . . . she would never forgive me. Humiliation is her greatest fear. My place in the community determines her place. At its best, this works beautifully. I've made her an important woman in town. If I get caught up in some tawdry scandal, however, she'll lose that place of importance. She'll become a figure of pity and shame. I honestly think she would sooner forgive me if I beat her.

Besides, it's not just Penny who would listen to Gary. I told him everyone would believe me, but that was bluster. Yes, many people love and respect me. And yes, many of them would stand beside me, no matter what anyone else said.

But I have my enemies, too, even among the elders of our church. The chairman of the deacons, Brother Amos, would entertain any slander laid against me. I cringe every time he rises to his feet in the middle of a business meeting and calls out from his pew, "Brother Weatherford, may I say a few words the Lord has laid on my heart?" Could I ever possibly say no? Could I ever possibly suggest that not every idea that pops into that old man's head was put there by the Almighty? No, of course not. So Amos stands there, with one hand jangling the car keys in his pocket while he delivers an oration in stentorian tones fit for the Gettysburg Address. And what has the Lord laid on his heart? Always the same thing. Always that the preacher is wrong, every time. The Lord has never told Amos that I did something right. To imagine him standing up in the middle of church and uttering the words "Gary Doane" makes me nauseous again.

And then, of course, there are all the people who would benefit from my public humiliation. I'm sure that the folks in the wet coalition would leap at the chance to point out my hypocrisy. The only thing Amos has in common with someone like Brian Harten is that they would both love to see me fall on my face.

I would be the local scandal, and my wife and children would be swamped in humiliation. And these days every local scandal has the potential to become a national one. I'm God's representative, called by him to proclaim the cross of Christ, and the world loves to see a man of the cross brought down by his own weakness.

It would be better if I'd died in my sleep last night.

I lower my face to the carpet, and I try to cry. I've cried many tears into the carpet of this room. Tears of misery and tears of exultation, all wept as I beseeched the Lord for one person or another. But I cannot weep for myself now. I cannot pray for myself.

I am too ashamed to face God.

⸻

Breakfast is served. Penny and the kids have prepared quite a feast. We hold hands as I say grace, and then, as we settle down to eat, the cacophony of voices rises around the table.

The older children discuss college. Mary talks about a history class she's enjoying, her favorite class of her freshman year, in fact.

Matthew seizes on this to critique the way our secular universities teach history. "It's worse than how they teach science," he says.

"Nothing," Mark says, "is worse than how they teach science." His voice slurs the *r* in *worse* to an *l*, a result of the cognitive damage he suffered at birth. My poor son. Though he still deals with a significant learning disability, he is pursuing a degree in cyber security from an online school, and he's been talking recently about moving out on his own. That would make things easier on us, but we worry about him heading out into the world.

Johnny, who has been sulking since I castigated him earlier, warms to the science topic, intuiting a way to return to my good favor. "Dad, how could people think we come from monkeys?"

"I don't know, son. Hitler said if you want to get people to believe a lie, you just keep repeating it. The secularists keep repeating the whole evolution thing, and people just accept it uncritically. They hear learned men with impressive degrees holding forth about monkeys and fossils or whatever, and they think, 'Well, I don't get it, but I guess it must all make sense, if these smart guys believe it.'"

Johnny shakes his head dramatically and turns to his little sister and says, "Monkeys . . ."

Ruth giggles and eats some bacon.

I smile at them. I don't have much of an appetite, so I merely sip some coffee.

Matthew says, "Well, at the college level, the problem's tenure. These wheezy old sixties liberals clogging up the academy—they're the fossils we should really be worried about."

For Matthew, everything is political. He's about to graduate from the University of Arkansas with a degree in Political Science—or Poli Sci, as he insists on calling it—and he's interested in going into politics himself. He expressed an interest in politics from an early age, even becoming president of the Young Republicans chapter in his high school, but his rage at Obama's reelection in 2012 fueled the fire of his ambition as nothing ever has. We're a family that discusses political matters, and I've never shied away from taking a stand on controversial issues in the pulpit. But I am a little wary of Matthew's obsession with the political. Still, while I fear the cost of him being too involved in the grimy world of politics, I am certain he would be a good leader.

I look around the table, at the faces of my bright and beautiful children. I labor to draw my breath. My chest feels tight. I close my eyes to concentrate, to find another breath.

"Richard, are you okay?" Penny asks.

I nod.

"You sure, Dad?" Matthew says.

"I'm fine." I reach for my glass of water and knock it over.

Mary puts her hand on mine. "Dad?"

"Perhaps I should lie down," I say. I find some air. I open my eyes.

Penny is at my side, her hand on my shoulder. "Are you okay?" She feels my face. "You're clammy. And you're sweating."

Worry covers all their faces. I've never seen this before, my wife and all five of my children staring at me this way. Poor Mark looks scared.

I attempt to smile. Sweat drips onto my glasses. I try to wipe it away and it smears my vision. "Perhaps I should lie down." I reach for Mary's glass and drink her water. "I'm fine."

They continue to stare at me. Matthew gets up and reaches for my arm to help me, but I affectionately swat his hand away and tell him, "I'm fine, I'm fine. You all stop making a fuss about it. Finish breakfast. I'm going to have a quick nap. I got up too early and had too much coffee. Just need to lie down."

Penny tells them all, "You heard him. Finish up."

She follows me down the hall and up the stairs. We don't say a word until we get in the bedroom and the door is closed.

I take off my glasses and lie down, and she asks, "Is it your chest?"

I rest my feet on the bed, and she starts pulling off my shoes.

"I'm fine," I say.

"Richard, don't be stubborn. Tell me what's wrong."

She sits down beside me.

I close my eyes so I don't have to look at her concerned and somewhat accusatory face.

"I felt suddenly dizzy, light-headed, and I had a little trouble breathing. It's nothing."

"It's not nothing to have breathing problems," she protests. "You should see Dr. Ritter."

I want to end this conversation, and I want her to leave. I learned long ago that the quickest way to get her to leave is to agree with everything she's saying. "Yes. Of course. I'll call first thing Monday morning."

"You sure you don't want to see someone right now?"

"I'm fine, really. I was dizzy for a second, but I'm okay now. My heart rate is fine. I'm sitting here talking to you, so my breathing is fine. I'll call Monday."

"*I'll* call Monday. Can't trust you to do it yourself."

"Thank you, dear."

"I'm going to let you rest."

"Thank you, dear."

"Is there anything I can get you?"

"You could close the blinds and pull the curtains."

She closes off the windows and then kisses my forehead. I don't open my eyes until the door shuts behind her and her footsteps move down the hallway.

It's mostly dark in the room, but resilient slivers of light slash out from the edges of the windows and strike across the wall. I pull the bed's comforter over my head and twist around until I'm encased in a black cocoon. I settle into the comfortable darkness. I can see nothing. I can feel only my breath. It's as if I have no body, as if I'm merely the breath that God himself breathed into Adam.

But the dark isn't a respite for long. The thoughts come. The regrets.

How could I have been so foolish? Satan comes cloaked as an angel of light; 2 Corinthians 11:14 tells us that. But I never thought Gary was an angel of light, did I? *I* was supposed to be the angel of light. His father was upset because Gary had flunked out of college. And the concern wasn't just about wasted tuition money or a stunted future; his parents were afraid that Gary might hurt himself. I was supposed to help.

How did that all go wrong? Was I always looking for someone like him? Nothing like this has happened to me before.

What about the man in Asheville?

No, the man in Asheville was an insane moment of weakness, fifteen years ago. That was about the abnegation of my whole self—Richard the man, the husband, the father, the Christian. The whole experience was traumatic, some stranger fucking me—I don't like that word, but there really is no other word for it—fucking me with conquest in his eyes, and after he had gone, I was in the motel shower, shaking and bleeding, more alone than I had ever been in my life.

I hated myself for it. I repented of it through tears. It was so traumatic that I thought I had been cured of the impulse.

But then one day Gary looked at me and didn't look away. We are nothing alike, our lives are nothing alike, but when he looked at me, I felt stripped of my defenses. Helpless. Exposed.

What did he see? I don't know, but I learned many years ago that there's nothing romantic at the center of man. I suspect there's nothing at the center of me except need and wanting. Maybe that's what he saw.

Gary was as much a pawn of the devil as I was, and I know I failed him. He gave me his trust, and I abused that trust. I didn't seduce him, though. I never meant for anything like this to happen. Neither did he. It just happened. The devil tricked us both. The devil promises the same easy solution to every problem, the same patch for every breach: do what you want.

I did. I fed my wanting.

So, yes, I was tricked, but I can't hide behind that. God is a mystery, but the devil is not. In all the ways that matter, I knew what I was doing. Certainly, I was clearheaded enough to orchestrate our interactions. I didn't want it to be like that night in Asheville. I wanted it to be playful and light. Fun. I wanted to watch him pleasure himself, my adolescent pornographic fantasies made flesh. Mostly, though, I wanted him to watch me, to see me. I wanted a man to witness my pleasure.

Or did I just want a witness to my depravity? Is there any real pleasure in this world without depravity? I'm not sure that there is, unless it's the ecstasy of finally shaking off the shackles of the flesh.

Eventually, I don't know after how long, there is a knock at the door. I unpeel myself from the cocoon and say, "Yes?"

The door opens. Penny says, "Sweetheart, Randy Ellis is here. He wants to talk to you about—"

"About the dry vote. Right. Tell him I'll be down."

"Are you sure, honey? I can tell him—"

"No, no. Don't be silly. I feel rested and much better."

She stares at me a moment, says nothing, and retreats.

I get up and walk over to the windows and throw open the curtains. The radiance of the day overwhelms my eyes, and I have to look away.

I slip on my shoes, pat down my hair, and walk downstairs.

Randy is in the kitchen talking with Matthew about Obama's foreign policy. Randy's wearing jeans held up by suspenders over a gray T-shirt that reads ONE NATION UNDER GOD, which accurately summarizes his views on all political matters.

When Matthew sees me, he says, "Feeling better, Dad?"

Randy pushes the sweaty Razorback ballcap back on his head. "You feeling poorly, Brother Richard?"

I wave it away. "Small headache. Penny acts like such a thing is the end of the world. Matthew takes after her, I guess."

The comment could hardly be more cutting to Matthew. While he loves his mother, he's always been rather uncomfortable with her position of authority within the family. Even as a small boy, he seemed to resent her power over him. He respects her as his mother, as a nurturer, but not as an authority. He aspires—as all my boys do—to be like me, and I think he's always felt that Penny was something of a usurper to the role of second-in-command of the family.

He tries to smile and roll with this slap, but the brightness in his face goes out. Now he knows he should be more circumspect.

While Matthew retreats, Randy—affable, good-natured Randy Ellis—is wholly unaware that anything has happened. He just rubs his big belly.

I ask him, "You get Patricia's Whopper yet?"

"Not yet. Get it on the way home."

With their sons grown and out of the house, Randy and his wife, Denise, live alone with an obese cocker spaniel named Patricia, and every day, Randy buys her a Whopper from Burger King.

As I walk him to my office, I ask, "Tell me something, you ever feed her a Big Mac, just to mix it up?"

He shrugs. "She don't like McDonald's."

We laugh about that, and I shut the office door.

"What's the news, Brother Randy?"

My desk faces the window, so I spin my chair around to face him. He takes the chair by my bookshelf. He starts to cross his legs, but his belly gets in the way. Instead, he grips his knees with his hands.

His face is serious, more serious than I've seen it in a while. "Well, I been talking to the folks on the quorum court, like you asked," he says.

"You talk to the Methodists?"

"I sure did. Tubb and Carter are both on board."

"That's encouraging news."

He asks, "That's the ball game, ain't it? I mean, if Tubb and Carter vote no, then there's no way a wet vote gets brought to the ballot. Or are you still concerned?"

"Well, it's fantastic news," I tell him. "No doubt about it. The wets are already in a shaky position, and without the Methodists, their odds just got a lot worse. But remember, the ball game's not over until they shut off the scoreboard and everybody goes home. Let's see how it plays out."

Randy takes a deep breath, a heavy breath. "You know, Brother Richard," he says, "I really appreciate you bringing me in on this deal."

I'm surprised by his somberness. "Of course, brother," I say. "I'm thankful for all your help."

He nods and clears his throat. "What I mean is . . . I just mean, and I don't know if you realize this, but tomorrow is the eighth anniversary of the first time I set foot in church."

"Has it been that long? I didn't realize."

He clears his throat again. "Well, I won't ever forget it. Denise dragged me in eight years ago." He smiles. "'It's Easter,' she said. 'Get your butt up. We're going to church.'"

"I know she'd been praying for you for a while, Randy."

"That's right, and she brought me to service and I heard you preach and it changed my life."

"Well," I say, "the Lord changed your life. I just tried to relay his message."

"You did his will, like always, and it turned me around. I quit drinking that week. I thought it would kill me. Now, though, I don't miss it at all."

"Praise the Lord."

"Praise the Lord," he repeats. "That's why I'm so proud to stand with you against this wet vote, Brother Richard. Stopping this thing from happening . . . I tell you, it feels pretty good. We can't have this."

"No, we can't."

"I just wish," he says, stumbling a bit, "just wish I'd quit sooner. Maybe my boys would be in a better place." He stares down at his thick hands.

I might have known that this was what was on his mind. His sons, Carl and Bobby, were both in high school when Randy was saved. Perhaps the hardest thing for a born-again Christian to do is to reintroduce himself to his family, particularly his children. It's not simply that you're telling your kids that you've changed; you're telling them your sins have been forgiven by a higher power. Some people, to put it mildly, do not want to hear that, particularly children. Children like to think of themselves as the only ones qualified to judge their parents. By his own accounting, before he got saved, Randy had been an imperfect father, given to casual drunkenness on one hand and a heavy-handed discipline on the other. When he came home that Easter and announced that he'd been saved, his boys reacted with extreme skepticism. And when he began to curtail their freedoms—forbidding secular music in the house, banishing alcohol and cigarettes, vetting their friends—their skepticism turned into angry defiance. Randy and Denise reacted to this rebellion by doubling down on the restrictions, forcing the boys to attend church for the first time in their lives. Bobby, only fifteen or so, grudgingly went along. Carl, eighteen and about to graduate, simply left home and didn't come back.

Now the boys are both in their twenties, and both are adrift. Bobby still lives in town, working second shift at the chicken plant and living with some meth addict in her forties. Carl, somewhere down in Little Rock, is lost to drugs. In a sense, it strikes me, Randy's salvation came at the cost of his family.

I ask, "Did something happen?"

"Well, Carl got shot." He says it simply, without inflection, as if he were telling me his son had lost his job.

I'm staggered. "Good Lord, Randy. Is he okay?"

"Yeah. Shot in the leg. He called us last night. Denise went down there this morning. She called me before I come over here. Says he's okay."

"What happened?"

"He was doing some kind of deal. You know he lives in Southwest Little Rock. You know what that means."

"Drugs."

"Yeah. We know he sells them. Bobby told us that much. Well, yesterday afternoon Carl was sitting around his apartment with some guy, a friend of his, just hanging out. This guy's not there ten minutes when there's a knock on the door, and they answer it and a couple of black guys come in. I guess they knew the other guy, Carl's friend, like he'd invited them over. But then one of these black guys pulls a gun and tries to rob Carl. So Carl pulls his gun, 'cause of course he just happens to have his gun on him, and shots were exchanged. This is Carl's story, anyway, the story we got, and the story he gave to the police."

"What do you think the truth is?"

"I think Carl's a drug dealer and these guys tried to rob him."

"Okay. And Carl got hit in the leg?"

"Yeah. Tore up his thigh but missed the bone and arties. Lucky wound, all things considered."

"Anybody else hurt?"

"Well, yeah, he killed the guy with the gun."

"Wait, Carl killed a guy yesterday?"

"Yeah," Randy says, looking down at his hands.

"My Lord."

Randy nods.

"Are you okay?" I ask.

He shakes his head. "Reaping what I sowed, Richard. Plain and simple fact of it. You plant sin, you grow sin."

He puts a big hand to his face.

I reach over and put a hand on his shoulder. "I'm sorry, man."

He nods.

I squeeze his shoulder. "I'm just so sorry."

He drops his hand to his thigh and says, "I just don't know what to do, Brother Richard."

"It's hard to know what to do," I say. "But the first thing you got to do is to reach out to the Lord. He's there for you. He's listening. He's got a plan."

Randy stares into my carpet. "You know I want to believe that . . ."

"Romans 8: 'And we know that all things work together for the good of those that love God.' *All* things, brother."

"Yeah."

"It's never too late to pray, Randy. He's always listening."

He nods. "That's right. I'm gonna pray on it."

"I know you will. You want to pray on it right now?"

"Yessir. It'd mean the world to me if you'd do the praying, Brother Richard, if you'd take this to the Lord for me right now."

"Of course."

We bow our heads. I pray, "Dear Heavenly Father, we come to you today to ask that you protect Carl, that you heal his body, and that you heal his heart."

Randy's voice cracks as he prays, "Yes, Lord. Please."

"Bring him into the fold, dear Lord. Bring him home to his mother and father, bring him home to you. And touch Bobby, too, Lord. Bring this family together and heal them, Lord. Be with Randy and give him the wisdom and strength to lead his family to you."

"Yes," Randy prays.

"We know you'll do this, Lord, because you are the great healer."

"That's right," Randy whispers.

"And, Father, we thank you and praise your name for bringing Randy into the family of God. We praise you, and we thank you for these last eight years. For what you've done in his life and in Denise's life."

"Amen, amen," Randy whispers.

"We pray all of this in the holy name of Jesus. Amen."

"Amen," Randy says. He looks up at me with tears still in his eyes. "Thank you," he tells me. "Really, Richard, thank you."

I pat his big hands, still clasped together for prayer. "You're very welcome, my friend. And I'll tell you what, let's go see your boy on Monday. You and me. Do you think that would be a good idea?"

Randy nods. "Yes. Thank you so much."

"No need to thank me. I'm happy to do it. Maybe this is the moment the Lord has put before us."

"Could we keep this quiet until then, though? I'd appreciate you not telling no one about it."

"You sure you don't want the church to pray about it? I know our prayer warriors would have your back."

"I'd just as soon keep it quiet. I don't mind you telling Penny, of course. I just ain't in a hurry to have everyone know about this."

"Of course. You have my discretion."

He climbs to his feet, flicking the last tear off his cheek with his meaty fingers. His voice rises, signaling a shift in mood.

"You going up to the church later?"

"Yeah. I have to help out with the Easter program. Gotta go over my narration."

He smiles. "Long as I've known you, I don't know how you get up and talk in front of all them people."

I open the door and slap him on the back. "All part of the job. I reckon the Lord picks the talkers to do the talking."

Randy says, "Speaking of people talking, I heard something down at the cement place this morning. Someone said that Ray ain't quitting after all. He told them he was going to stay on."

"Really?"

"What I heard."

"Maybe that means Ray is bailing on Brian."

"That's what I thought. If Ray bails out, you figure Brian will throw in the towel?"

"No," I say, tapping my finger against my lips. "Brian's the one with the real fire in his belly. I always got the sense that Ray was just along for the ride. Brian was always the engine of that partnership."

Randy says, "Still, though, things sure don't look good for Harten."

"Sure don't."

As he steps onto our front porch, he says, "Okay, Brother Richard, see you tomorrow."

"Yep, see you then."

"And we can talk about going to see Carl on Monday," he says. "I'll know more then."

"Oh, yeah." I nod. "Of course."

Monday. How do I get to Monday?

As I watch him walk out to his truck, I can feel the nausea again.

I close the door and walk back to my office. I stop in the hallway, next to the wall of our family pictures.

How do I get to Monday?

Now is not the time to panic. Now is the time to work out how to make this work. Focus.

How do I get to Monday?

I go into my office, and as I'm sitting down, something Randy said comes back to me.

Things sure don't look good for Harten.

Brian Harten must be quite desperate right now. The vote is going to go against him. Everyone knows it. He has to know it, too.

He must hate me.

Yes, of course, he hates me.

But he must also be desperate.

I wonder how desperate.

FIVE BRIAN HARTEN

Roxie ain't happy to see me.

"It ain't your day to get the kids," she says.

"I know."

"Then why are you here?"

There's a truck in the driveway next to her car. I nod at it. "Whose truck?"

She leans against the doorway and crosses her arms. She's got on a blue tank top and the Captain America sweatpants that the kids got her a couple of Christmases ago.

"Jeff's."

"Who the fuck is Jeff?"

"Jeff is the guy who drives that truck."

"And why is Jeff's truck parked in your driveway? Where is Jeff?"

Roxie is kind of skinny, small tits, no hips. She's got freckles and brown hair and brown eyes. When we were married, I got kind of tired of having sex with her. No, not tired. I just got used to having sex with her. It was like driving to work, wasn't much new to see. Now though, with her arms crossed and her face scrunched up and shitty, I'm kinda turned on by her. Her neck looks so soft, and her hair is brushing across her freckled shoulders. If she wanted to have sex right now, I'd do it in a heartbeat.

But she ain't thinking about sex.

"It ain't none of your damn business who I see," she says. "We ain't married. I don't come around your house first thing in the morning asking you about who's having breakfast."

"He spent the night?"

"I'm fixin' to shut the door unless you got something else to say, Brian."

"I'm just saying, I think I got a right to know who's in there eating cereal with my babies."

"They're having bacon and eggs, and all you got to know is that he's my friend and he's here."

"Bacon and eggs. Since when do you make bacon and eggs for people?"

"Ugh." She shakes her head and starts to close the door, but I stop her.

"Okay. Hey, I ain't here for none of that, anyway. I came by to ask if I could borrow your car."

She stops and frowns and looks over my shoulder. "Where's your car?"

"Broke down."

"What's wrong with it?"

"Alternator, I think. I got to get it checked."

"Why you need to borrow my car?"

"I need to run over to Morrilton."

"Why?"

"You got to know my business?"

"If you want to borrow my car."

"I need to go see Tommy. He owes me money. I need to get the money so I can pay to get the car worked on."

"He gonna be in this early?"

"He usually comes in early on the weekends to get away from Carmen and Sarabeth. He'll do paperwork or make some calls or whatever. Half the time he's just sitting there watching TV."

She nods and grabs her purse from the coatrack and pulls out the keys. She holds on to them, though. "When will you be back?"

"What time is it?"

"Like ten thirty."

"I don't know. Noon, maybe one? Two at the latest."

"Two at the latest."

"Yeah."

She hands me the keys.

The floorboards are full of a bunch of crap. McDonald's wrappers and old comic books and pieces of the kids' schoolwork. Roxie's car has always looked like a rolling trash can. I never understood that. I keep my shit nice. That's the point of having it, ain't it? For it to be nice. Never made sense to me to buy a vehicle and then treat it like a dumpster.

Still, it feels good to be in a car and not to have to walk. I cross the Little Red River Bridge, pass the church, and I'm pointed out of town. Couldn't make this trip walking, that's for sure. Nice of Roxie to let me borrow it, I guess.

No, fuck that. She only let me borrow it so she could rub my face in it later. Today or tomorrow or a fucking year down the road—at some point that bitch is going to throw this back in my face.

Jeff. Who the fuck is Jeff? Not Jeff Black? No, couldn't be. Maybe Jeff Whatshisname who works at Walmart.

I don't know. Guess it don't matter. No use in getting jealous.

I ain't jealous anyway, not exactly. If *Jeff* wants to put up with Roxie's bullshit, better him than me.

I would love to fuck her, though. One last time.

Guess ol' Jeff is fucking her now.

Whatever.

Away from town, the highway curves into the trees. Trees, trees, trees. The north of Arkansas ain't nothing but trees. The bottom of the state ain't nothing but swamp. I prefer the trees, I guess, but sometimes I think I should have got out of here. Sure, I left Van Buren County, but where did I go? One county over. What good did that do me? Here I am, right back where I started. No money. No family. Driving my ex-wife's car on my way to see my ex-boss.

Real success story.

Tommy's Bar is closed, but his truck is out front next to the statue. He always parks next to the statue. Not enough that he built a goddamn statue to himself, he's gotta park next to it.

The statue is stupid-looking. Tommy tells everyone it's "cold cast bronze," but I was there when he bought the damn thing, and I know for a fact that it's just resin with some bronze powder mixed in. So, it's eight feet of bronzey-looking resin, on top of a four-foot concrete pedestal, and it's supposed to be Tommy in his prime, with a three-foot-long baseball bat propped up on his shoulder. It's a shitty statue, and it doesn't even look like him anymore since he got beer fat sitting on his ass behind the bar. When he was a high school baseball champ and got a college scholarship, he was lean and mean and eighteen. Now he's just another fat redneck.

He don't know it, though. He thinks he's the statue.

I park next to a couple of cars in the lot and go inside. The chairs are up on the tables, and Tommy is behind the bar. There's two girls at the bar with him. I don't know them. Maybe they're new waitresses. They're both young and pretty. One's Chinese, or Korean maybe. Don't see many Asian girls around here. Must be adopted.

They all look me over when I come in, and I see Tommy smile.

He leans back so far he almost bumps his head on the Louisville Slugger mounted on the wall. "Harten, my man. The entrepreneur returns." He's wearing beige cargo shorts and a tight pink polo shirt that makes him look like a big nipple.

"Hey, Tommy, what's up?"

The girls are sitting on barstools playing 21 with Tommy. They have pennies in front of them. He has dollars. I've seen him play this game with girls before—him betting dollars and them betting pennies. He just does it to show off. The girls never mind. Basically, he's paying them to hang around with him.

He says, "You know Ka and Britney?"

The girls smile at me. Ka is the Asian girl. Britney is a blonde.

"No." I nod at them. "What's up?"

They nod back and look at each other. Ain't sure what to make of me yet.

Tommy shuffles the cards. "What's shaking, Harten?"

"Oh, not much. Thought I'd come by to pick up my check."

"Check for what?"

"Paycheck."

He doesn't even look at me when he says, "Last I checked, you don't work here no more, Harten." He looks up at the girls and smiles. "Hey, 'Last I checked you ain't got no check.' That's a . . . whadaya call it? Like a rhyme?"

"A pun?" Ka says.

"Yeah, a pun."

I say, "You still owe me from last month."

"Last month?"

"Yeah."

He shuffles the cards, pulls one out, looks at it, slides it back in, and keeps shuffling.

The girls have stopped smiling. Ka looks at Britney. Britney keeps looking back and forth between me and Tommy.

"Last month," I say.

"Hm. How much you think I owe you for last month?"

"You don't know how much you owe people?"

"Yeah, yeah, I do. I do. Which is where I get confused, because I'm pretty sure that I don't owe you nothing. You quit before the end of the month."

"I worked, Tommy. You owe me three hundred bucks easy."

He puts down the cards on the counter and looks at me, his dumb-ass eyes squinting out from his fat face. "You didn't even show up to work that last day."

"I called Katy and let her know."

"You ain't supposed to call another employee; you're supposed to call me. You left me high and dry."

"I had shit I had to tend to."

"You up and quit on me over the phone by calling a waitress. That's some weak sauce, my friend. That dog don't hunt."

Ka looks nervous. Britney smiles.

"You still owe me, Tommy."

He shakes his head. "You left me in the lurch that night. I gotta deduct that."

"That ain't how it works."

"Plus, I had to pay someone else to pick up the shift."

"So? What's that got to do with—"

"So, I'd say that leaves us about even."

I don't really know what to say. I know this asshole is never going to pay me what he owes me. Tommy is a shitty boss to the people who work for him. And me? I'm just a guy who *used* to work for him.

I shake my head. I ask the girls, "Y'all just hire on here?"

They both stare at me.

"Do y'all work here?"

Ka nods.

"Then just keep in mind what you're seeing. This is who Tommy Weller is."

"Okay," Tommy says. "Why don't you get out of my bar?"

"Motherfucker owns four businesses," I tell the girls. "You know that? Course you do. He tells anybody who'll listen. Got that statue out front here of himself with a baseball bat. Which is hilarious since literally nobody in the state of Arkansas gives one warm shit about baseball. And where did he play baseball? Big leagues? No. Minor leagues? No. In *college*. Yeah, I mean, who the hell doesn't love college baseball?"

Tommy asks, "Where'd you play, Brian?"

I don't even look at him. I tell the girls, "He flunked out of college, by the way. He was there a year before he flunked out."

Tommy says, "And then I come back here and started four successful businesses, Brian. How many businesses you own?"

"I got one on the way."

"Is that right?"

"Yeah."

"Is that right?"

"Yes, it is."

"Ain't the way I heard it. Way I heard it is Van Buren County ain't gonna let you in there."

"We'll see about that."

Tommy smiles and says, "Yeah. We sure will."

I look between the three of them. Britney is barely keeping a lid on a laugh that's gonna let loose before I even hit the parking lot. Ka looks kind of horrified by the whole thing. And Tommy is grinning like he just yanked down my pants.

I turn around and stomp outside. I jump in Roxie's car like I'm about to tear out of there. But all I can do is sit and stare at the shadow of Tommy's big plaster baseball bat over the hood.

I press my thumb to my lips. I don't have anywhere to go. I don't have anyone to call. I'll drive back to Stock and drop off Roxie's car. And then I'll walk back to my apartment.

I put my head in my hands.

My phone buzzes. I rub my eyes and pull the phone out of my pocket. I recognize the number. Richard Weatherford. I called him last month to complain about something he said at a city council meeting. Maybe he's calling to return the favor.

"Hello," I say.

"Yes, hello. Is this Brian?"

"Yeah."

"Yes, Brian. This is, uh, this is Richard Weatherford. How are you?"

"I'm not too hot, Reverend. What can I do for you?"

"I was hoping we could talk."

"Okay."

"I was hoping we could talk together. In person. Today, preferably."

"What do you want to talk about? I'm busy."

"Well, it's about the upcoming vote."

"I'm not in the mood for another sermon on the evils of alcohol, Preacher."

"Yes, well, I'm not going to preach. At all. In fact, I was hoping we could talk about it."

There's something weird in his voice. He's never sounded like this. For a second, I'm not really sure it's him. "Okay . . ."

"I think you might want to hear what I have to say."

"Okay, then. Where? Your church?"

"Uh, no," he says. "What I have to say is rather sensitive. I wonder if we could meet somewhere we could have a discreet conversation."

"A discreet conversation."

"Yes."

"Where'd you have in mind?"

"You know the car wash down Huddo Road?"

"Yeah."

"I can be there in ten minutes."

"I'm out on the road," I say. "How about an hour?"

"An hour? Okay. Yes. An hour."

"I'll see you then."

"Brian, one more thing."

"Yeah."

"I'd appreciate it if you didn't mention this to anyone yet. Let's keep it under our hats, if you don't mind, until we have a chance to talk."

"Kinda sketchy, Preacher."

"No." He laughs, nervous. "No, nothing 'sketchy.' I'd just like a word with you."

We hang up, and I'm sitting there looking at the phone, thinking, *Now, what the hell does he want?*

SIX RICHARD WEATHERFORD

I've just hung up with Brian Harten when my phone buzzes in my hand. I jump because I assume it's Brian calling me back.

Instead, it's my father. I hang my head and groan.

I can't miss this call.

"Hey, Dad," I say.

I hear him settling into his armchair. "Well," he bellows, "how's it going?"

"Going well," I say. "All the kids are home for Easter."

"Yeah? That's good."

"We were sorry you couldn't make it down."

"Oh, you know I'm too busted up to travel. Y'all should come see me."

I try to laugh that off. "Dad, why do you always invite me to come visit at the only time of the year you know I can't come visit?"

"What do you mean?"

"Inviting me to come visit you on Easter is like inviting a groom to come visit on his wedding day."

"Well, I don't mean now, necessarily. Just, you know, one of these days."

This is the thing he says every time we talk. In response, I say the thing I say every time we talk.

"Yeah, we need to make it out to see you sometime. Right now, I'll tell you, I've really got a lot of things going on."

Dad chuckles. It's not mocking, but his amusement carries a hint of sarcasm. "That two-day work week running you ragged?"

My face gets hot, but I try to laugh with him. "You wouldn't believe how much I have on my plate, Dad."

"Oh, don't get sensitive. I know you do. Got all them kids to wrangle. Your mother and me could barely handle one. Speaking of your offspring, Matt graduated yet?"

"In a couple of months."

"He given any thought to what's next?"

"Well, it looks like he's going to grad school."

"Grad school? No kidding. For that political science thing?"

"Yes. He'll stay at U of A."

"Gonna be a politician, I guess."

"Time will tell. He's already made some good contacts."

"He wants to run for office one day, he should go into the service. None of these politicians have any military service anymore."

"I know."

"I do like ol' Trump, though."

"Yeah?"

"Sure. The Mexican border's got more holes than a piece of Swiss cheese. He's right about that. Got all kinds of people coming over every day and sponging off welfare, driving down the wages, having litters of kids. Somebody's got to put a stop to it."

"I'm holding out for Cruz."

"Ain't he Cuban or something?"

"Well, part Cuban, I think. He's a Southern Baptist."

"That's good."

"What else is new with you, Dad?"

He laughs. "I'm old, son. When you're old, everything is new, and nothing is. My right hand is just about done. That's the latest development."

"What do you mean?"

"Well, I only got one finger on that hand that works, my pinkie. And what can you do with that? The fingers that do all the real work, they ain't worth a damn. They've gone stiff as a board."

"Did you go to the doctor?"

"Next time you send up a prayer, say a word for my hand."

"I will. Did you see a doctor, though?"

"Oh sure, but these VA doctors don't know nothing. This little ol' gal that was working on me told me they could chop off the fingers if I wanted. You believe that? I said, 'Well, do you need to?' and she said, no, they ain't going to kill me or nothing. So I told her, 'Well, darlin', I'd just as soon keep my fingers, if it's all the same to you. They're useless, but they're mine.' These doctors don't know nothing."

"But, Dad, what did they say was wrong? Is it complications from the diabetes?"

"Oh, well, the diabetes is probably in there somewheres, I reckon, but there's also that nerve damage in my arm, too, from the time I rolled my jeep in the service. Plus, I got the osteoarthritis. So that's another factor. But that's the way it goes. When you start getting old, it's always something. And once you start getting really old, it's always ten different things. I'm so beat up now, it's getting hard to remember a time when I felt whole."

"You been praying about it?"

"Oh, the Lord's got better things to think about than my old broke-down body. I'm getting old, that's all. No use bothering God about it."

"I'm not sure that's true . . ."

"Don't preach at me, son."

"How about Scripture? You reading your Bible?"

"I don't have to read it. I know it's true. That's all that matters."

"Well, are you at least going to church, Dad?"

"Oh, sure. I go just about every Sunday."

"Well, I'm glad to hear that, at least."

"I don't like the new music guy, though."

"Why not?"

"Well, he gets up there with a guitar. Got a kid on drums, one on bass. I mean, they're okay, but guitars and drums in a church? I thought church was for pianos and organs, not rock and roll."

"You know, a lot of churches have praise bands these days. Almost all the big churches do."

"Well, your granddaddy only believed in two things—the United States Marine Corps and the Southern Baptist Convention—and if he'd lived long enough to see some longhair beating drums on a Sunday morning, I think he would have shot somebody."

We both laugh at that, and I say, "I know what you mean, Dad, but there's nothing in the Bible that mandates the playing of an organ to praise the Lord."

"If you say so. Y'all don't have that Christian rock-n-roll at your church, do you?"

"Heaven forbid. If I let somebody put drums on the stage, Amos Pettibone would lead people to my house with torches and pitchforks. Maybe that's why I can't get our membership above three hundred."

"Three hundred ain't bad."

"I guess not." I think of his two-day-work-week comment earlier, and I add, "Three hundred keeps me plenty busy. I do my visitations on Monday. I do a senior adult Bible study every Tuesday morning, plus I do the business meetings every month, in addition to writing two sermons for the Sunday services and the Bible study on Wednesday night."

"Well," he says with the tone he uses to cue the end of a call, "I reckon I should let you get back to it. Sounds like you got a lot going on. You say hi to everybody for me."

"I don't have to run this minute . . ."

"You tell Penny I said hello."

"Okay, Dad."

"Okay, son."

We hang up, and that's it for my father until Christmas.

~⊁~

When it's time to leave, I walk into the kitchen where Penny is talking to Mary and Ruth. My girls.

Penny is sitting on a barstool by the island, her legs crossed, coffee in her hand. Mary and Ruth are sitting on the kitchen counter—a practice I long ago gave up trying to discourage when I realized that I had no support from Penny.

When Ruth sees me, she jumps down from the counter and runs over and hugs my waist. Although she's every bit the cute little nine-year-old girl, of all the children she is the one who most looks like me. The resemblance is right there in the center of our faces. We have the same prominent nose, thick lips, and big teeth. As they say, I couldn't lose her in a crowd.

I pat her back. "Hello, my daughter."

"Hello, my father. Can I go to Scarlett's house?"

"I don't know, *can* you?"

"*May* I go to Scarlett's house?"

"Did you ask your mother?"

"I did."

"And what did she say?"

"To ask you."

"Then yes. I can drive you, too."

Ruth cheers and runs upstairs.

"Richard . . ." Penny gives me the raised-eyebrow look that is supposed to trigger a recollection of the obvious, but I have no idea what the obvious is supposed to be here.

"What?" I say.

"All the children are home. I thought we were going to hang out as a family."

"Dear, if you wanted her to stay home, you should have told her so yourself."

"But you are the beloved head of our household."

"Since when?"

"Oh, hardy har har," Penny says, sipping her coffee.

Mary smiles at that. The children have always appreciated our parental banter. When we were younger, it had more of a sharpness to it, more anger, more frustration. Over the years, it's softened considerably into playful bickering, enough so that I can make these little jokes about abdicating my authority. It's understood, of course, that mine is the final word. But I have attempted, metaphorically speaking, to wear that crown a little lightly.

"Are you feeling better, Dad?" Mary asks.

"Yes. Thanks for asking."

"He's going to see the doctor on Monday for a checkup," Penny says.

I wave in an exaggerated way. "Meh, doctors. I don't need their black magic."

"He's joking," Penny tells our daughter, "but you know I'll have to drag him in there on Monday. Just like a man. They all think they're too tough to see a doctor."

"That's me. Tough guy."

"Were you talking to someone just now?" Penny asks. "I thought I heard you on the phone."

"My father called."

"Oh."

Mary says, "How's Grandpa?"

I shrug. "As constant as the North Star."

She smiles. "Did he ask you why Matt's not joining the Marine Corps?"

"It might have come up, yes."

"Did he bring up that you should have joined the Corps?"

"It must have slipped his mind this time."

Although my father was proud of me for going into the ministry, he was disappointed that I hadn't followed him into the Marine Corps. I flirted with the idea, even met with a silver-tongued recruiter who offered me the world on a platter, but I felt compelled to follow the Lord instead. Dad even pushed the idea of my becoming a chaplain. If I'd had the decision to make after 9/11, I'm certain I would have gone into the Marines like my father wanted, but in the early nineties, I legitimately thought I could do more good in the world as a minister. Besides, I'd seen enough of the military life through my father to know that I sought higher ground.

Ruth comes downstairs.

I ask, "You ready, Baby Ruth?"

"Daddy, I'm too old to be called Baby Ruth."

"My daughter, you will never to be too old to be my Baby Ruth."

She makes a production of rolling her eyes and shrugging. "Okay then. I'm ready to go."

"Okay."

"You're coming right back?" Penny asks.

"What?"

"I said, you're coming right back, right?"

"Why do you ask?"

"I was just wondering."

"Yes," I say, a little irritated. "I'm coming right back."

She sips her coffee and turns away from me. "Just don't want you to run away from home."

—★—

Scarlett's house is five minutes from the car wash. After I drop off Ruth, I turn onto Huddo Road.

Penny's somewhat odd comment lingers in my mind, though she's always been given to making little caustic remarks. I can think of no reason she would have to be suspicious of me today, but I can tell something's bothering her. After twenty-four years of marriage, I can always feel when the pressure is building beneath her strange silences and offhanded comments.

It took us a long time to understand each other. When we first began dating in college, I was constantly baffled by how fervently she worshipped her parents. She'd been their miracle baby, their only child after three miscarriages, and their family was intensely close. Truth be told, though, she'd created a false idol out of her parents. Her worship of them lasted into the first decade of our marriage and, aside from money, was the source of most of our marital problems. Simply put, she wanted me to be a copy of her father. Dan was a good man, but I'd just crawled out from under the influence of my own father, and I didn't need a new template. It took Penny years to come to terms with the fact that the man she married was never going to be her father, years for her to finally accept that the Lord brought us together for a reason. Certainly, he has blessed us with children. She sees as well as I do the hand of Providence in that. Still, if I know her heart the way I think I do, I know she'll always place me somewhere just below her father when it comes to measuring the worth of a man.

The oddity of that, of course, is that I'm more successful than Dan ever was. I have the bigger house, the more impressive job. And not that it's about numbers, but I have five children, and he, like my father, only had one.

Yet I can feel my face redden as I reflect that neither Dan nor my father ever did what I'm about to do. Suddenly, I'm so hot, I have to roll down the window to get some fresh air.

For all his faults, Dad never did what I'm doing. But he never had this kind of responsibility, either. He never had to protect an entire church.

After passing a few more houses and a couple of old barns, I turn off Huddo to follow a small, arrow-shaped sign for the car wash. I climb a shaded gravel road up to two rickety aluminum stalls at the top of a hill, where I find Brian Harten waiting for me in his car.

As I pull into the vacant stall, Harten walks around, his hair tousled in the wind. Stepping out of the minivan, I glance toward the road. Aside from glimpses of Huddo Road trailing off into the distance, the swaying trees ringing the hill obscure the view.

"Thank you for meeting me," I tell him.

"Why are we here?"

He's a young man, Brian Harten. Perhaps thirty or so. His clothes have a slept-in look, and his matted brown hair appears unwashed. Despite the cool winds coming through the trees, sweat beads his bland face and scruffy chin.

I say, "I wanted to talk to you about our . . . About the situation with the upcoming vote."

"Yeah," he says, "but why the fuck are we meeting way out here?"

"Because I wanted to talk to you in private."

"Okay, well, here we are. So what do you want to say?"

"First, you and I both know that the quorum's going to go against you."

"You don't know that."

"Yes, I do. And so do you. There are too many people around here who want Van Buren County to stay dry."

"Because you riled them up."

"Well, whatever the politics of the thing, it wasn't personal, Brian, I can tell you that. I'm actually really impressed by you. No, I mean it. Although we've been at opposite ends of this thing, I know you're a sharp, motivated young man with enormous potential. Anyone can see that."

"That's a huge relief, Preacher. I thought you were ruining my life because you didn't like me."

"If I hurt you, Brian, it wasn't intentional. I always liked you. In fact, I wanted to talk to you today because I want to see if I can help you."

"What does that mean? Help me with what?"

"Well, I know you've got a lot tied up in your store. A lot invested in its success."

"Yeah . . ."

"And I've given it some thought . . . What if I could help things go your way?"

"What do you mean?"

"Like you said, I'm a big reason why this vote is going to go against you. What if I turned it around? What if I could help you get the wet ordinance put on a special ballot?"

He just stares at me a moment before he says, "What?"

"I have a situation of my own. And I need some assistance. I think you could help me."

"What kind of assistance are we talking about?"

I have to force a breath up from my chest before I can bring myself to say, "Financial."

"You're shaking me down."

"I wouldn't call it that. I'm coming to you with a proposition. I can help the vote go your way."

"In exchange for some money."

"Well . . ."

"That's a shakedown. What you just said—that's like the legal definition of a shakedown."

I put my shoulders back and try to stand up straighter. "Call it what you will—what would you say to my proposition?"

"I would say that I don't have any money."

I blink at that. "Oh."

Wind rattles the stalls.

"I'm poor," he says. "Did you not realize that? You're out here trying to extort money from a poor man."

"I just thought—"

"How much you want?"

"I need thirty thousand dollars."

He blinks, opens his mouth to speak, but can't find the words. Finally, he brings himself to say, "I don't have anything, Preacher. I'm driving my ex-wife's car. I can't even pay child support. All my prospects for cash are tied up in the store . . . and you drag me out here to the fucking car wash to ask me for thirty thousand dollars. I mean, I'd be pissed off right now if I wasn't so fucking dumbfounded."

I look over at the dripping stalls. I don't know how to respond to him. I cross my arms, but it feels awkward, so I drop them to my sides.

"Why," he says, "didn't you come to me two months ago with this deal? I mean, why wait until I'm going bankrupt?"

"I didn't need it two months ago. I need it now."

"How come you don't just pray for the money?"

I let that go.

He stares at me. "What's to keep me from telling everybody about this?"

I nod as if we're just discussing possibilities. "Do you think anyone would believe you?"

"Yeah, I bet they would."

"I think it'd be a bad bet to assume that anyone would believe you."

"Why?"

"Because I'm a pillar of the community and the pastor of the biggest church in this county. And while I need some money off the books, I'm doing well financially—probably one of the better-off people around here. That's who I am. You, though, you're broke. You just said so yourself. You're a guy sliding into bankruptcy because he tried to open a liquor store in a dry county. That's who you are. No one would believe that *I* would come to *you* for money. And no one would believe that I offered to help you turn the county wet. People would just assume you were trying to smear me out of spite."

He shakes his head and starts to leave.

I grab his arm. "Wait."

"Get the fuck off me, man," he barks, shoving me away.

I stumble back against the minivan. To stop him from leaving, I say, "I can help you get your store."

That stops him.

Regaining my balance, I ask, "That's the bottom line, isn't it? If you leave here, what do you get? Think about it. What do you get? Nothing. If you went out there this afternoon and trashed me to everybody in town, it wouldn't get you any closer to getting your store."

"Why not?"

"Because if I go down in disgrace today, it won't flip a single vote on the quorum court for you. But if we work together, I *can* help you."

"How you can't just suddenly go, 'Never mind. Now I'm supporting the wet vote.'"

I shake my head. "What you never understood," I tell him, "was that you were never going to get anywhere in this fight once you made it about wet versus dry. Once you said it was about the freedom to buy a drink, you made it a moral issue. And the dry side was always going to win the moral argument. We had doctrine and tradition in our corner. But the dry side isn't some monolith. It's made up of a lot of different people. Different ideas. Different priorities, economic and otherwise. I know where the fracture points are in that coalition. Good Lord, do I. I had to keep them all together. I guarantee you that there are votes to be had on the quorum court just by driving a wedge between Tonya Hooper and John Floyd Jr. over the shale gas debate, between the appropriations for water quality control and the fight for more extraction permits. I bet you didn't know that . . . Of course not. Forgive me for saying this, Brian, but you're in over your head. You are. But I can do it. You said so yourself that I was the one who made this vote go against you. Well, I promise you I can make the vote go *for* you just as easily."

He says, "Okay then, how about you do that for me. You help the vote go my way, and I'll keep this meeting quiet."

"I still need the money."

"And I still don't got any money, Preacher."

"It's a condition, Brian. I have to have it. If I don't get this thirty grand, off the books, as soon as possible, then I can't help either one of us. Get me the money, and I can turn the vote around for you."

"And how long would it take you to turn the vote around?"

"I don't know. Could be a few months. Could be less."

"A few months? I'm about to lose my ass today."

"It could be less. Either way, if you can hold on, Brian, I can turn the vote around."

"And you'd do that?"

"Yes. Look at it this way, Brian: if you get me this money, then I have no choice. I'll *have* to help you get the measure on the ballot."

He steps away from me. One step.

I shut up because I can tell he's thinking. He's thinking, and I know the look in his eyes. Like any natural-born salesman, I know when I have someone. God forgive me, but it's a look I know because I've seen it many times when leading people to the Lord. No offer of salvation seems implausible to a man desperate to be saved.

He bites his lip. He rubs his forehead.

"I still don't have any money . . ."

I nod.

I let him come to it on his own.

"But," he says finally, drawing a deep breath, "I might know how I can get some."

SEVEN PENNY WEATHERFORD

I walk into the laundry room and take some clothes out of the dryer, fold them, and place them in a basket. I asked Matthew and Mary to bring home whatever they wanted washed this weekend, and I find their dirty clothes and linen in Big Blue. I run a mixed load of their coloreds, and then I take the basket of clean clothes upstairs.

When Matthew and Mary went off to college, Johnny and Ruth took over their bedrooms. When the older kids are back from school, they share the rooms with the young ones, and I'm happy with how this arrangement has worked out. Johnny's always worshiped Matthew, and Ruth treats Mary like a vacationing celebrity, so it's rather like the older ones are mentoring the younger ones. The only person left with a bedroom of his own in this house is Mark, and he seems content to be by himself.

He's sitting on his bed right now listening to Elvis Presley sing gospel. This interest in Elvis's gospel recordings is new. Mark's musical tastes have always run toward Christian rock and pop, but he tends to discover a single group and get locked into it and obsessed with it exclusively for months or years on end. Hillsong. MercyMe. Casting Crowns. He doesn't listen to a million bands, but he'll listen to one band a million times. I think this intense focus has something to do with his desire to understand the world around him. He wants a full accounting of things. Of our children, he's the only one who does prodigious Bible study. I think it might be the only book he's ever read, but he reads it almost every day.

And now he's obsessed with Elvis.

Richard never noticed the musical quirks of our second child, and when I pointed them out to him, he said, "That's right. I guess he's a completist." He thought it about it a moment more and said, "That's good. Shows dedication."

This has been our way as parents, I think. I observe our children and explain them to Richard, and he passes a judgment.

Elvis is singing a song I don't know. It's a big production number.

"I have your clean clothes," I say, placing the stack at the foot of Mark's bed.

"Thank you, Mama," he says. Of the children, he's the only one who calls me Mama. When they were little, Matthew hated it. He thought it sounded babyish, and he demanded that Mary address me as "Mom" the same way he did. Mary, who loved both her brothers but saw that Matthew was dominant, acquiesced. So "Mama" has stayed a thing between Mark and me.

"What song is this?" I ask, sitting down.

"'Reach Out to Jesus,'" he says.

"I don't know it. It's pretty."

He nods.

"You like Elvis, Mama?"

I shrug. "Sure. Who doesn't?"

He nods. The song crescendos. The next song is a jumpy piano number.

"You've been listening to a lot of Elvis lately," I say. "Why?"

"They call him the king of rock and roll."

"Yeah."

"But he does gospel. Did you know that?"

"I knew he did some."

"He does a lot. I didn't know that. I thought he just did secular." He mangles the word *secular*. I don't often hear his speech impediment, but secular has a *u* in the middle as well as both an *l* and an *r*, so his pronunciation is a clunky chain of incorrect sounds. I don't correct it. Richard still corrects Mark's pronunciation sometimes, even now that he's on the verge of turning twenty-one, but I don't see the point. Mark has other things to contend with. Torturing him over the letter *r* seems pointless and even a little cruel.

"Did you know he was a twin?" Mark asks.

"Who?"

"Elvis."

"Elvis had a twin?"

"At birth, but something went wrong in his mama's belly and the baby died."

I stare at my boy a moment. He's a sensitive soul, my second born. There's so much locked inside him that he can't get to, yet he feels things so deeply sometimes. He's never been able to make sense of what happened to him when he was born. I've explained to him that he stopped breathing for a time, and that hurt him, but God had a plan and delivered the perfect Mark to us. Sometimes I think he believes me, looks in my eyes and knows I'm telling him the truth. Other times I worry that he sees a different idea in my husband's eyes.

Penny, that's an awful thing to think . . .

I shake my head and stand up. I can be so unkind to Richard.

I kiss Mark's forehead, pick up my clothes basket, and carry it to my bedroom. I hang up some of my blouses. I pull out a couple of Richard's folded dress shirts. I hang up two that he might want to wear tomorrow and place the rest in his dresser drawer.

I put away my underwear. Then his.

How odd that I touch his clothes but never touch him. I know the most intimate details of his body, yet he's hidden that body from me for years. Why is he so ashamed?

I take a deep breath, as if I've just run up a hill. I know he's not ashamed of his body. He's stayed fit, like his father. Neither of them has ever been the beer-drinking type, nor have either of them ever compensated for the lack of alcohol by becoming sugar junkies. At forty-six, Richard's among the fittest men in our church. He's proud of that fact. He'll make little comments about some of our heavier members. Even somebody like Randy, whom he loves, Richard will joke around with him, teasing him about his weight. I don't think Randy thinks anything of it, but I know why Richard does it. He just likes to remind people of their faults. He can't help it. It's the first thing he looks for when he meets someone new.

I walk into our bathroom to put away some towels, and I'm stopped by my reflection in the vanity. How odd that they call it a vanity. I have no vanity as I stare at myself. I've kept in reasonable shape. I'm not much larger than I was when we got married. I was never thin, and I'm not fat. I've always been a healthy average. But when I lift up my shirt, my midsection looks sixty or seventy years old, battle-scarred from five pregnancies and one late-term miscarriage. My belly will never be the same, a messy patchwork of loose flesh and C-section scars.

I thought of having it fixed, but the only thing I can imagine that would repulse Richard more than my body would be the cost of a surgery or two to fix it.

My body. I hold up my hand and stare at the veins running through my palms. I stare at the thick white scar at the base of my right thumb. I don't know how the scar got there; it's just something that happened to me before I reached an age where I could remember things. How odd that we're bodies and people at the same time. I stare at myself in the mirror again. It seems like most of life is about trying to figure out how to be both a body and a person.

As I finish putting away the towels, my phone buzzes on the counter. I reach for it, thinking it might be Richard, but it's a number I haven't seen in years. Sandy Loomis. For a moment, I just stare at her name. Then I answer.

"Hello?"

"Penny, it's Sandy Hadden."

Her maiden name. She dropped Loomis when she divorced Gene, our music minister. He had to leave the ministry because of that.

"Well, hello, stranger," I say, trying to sound friendly. I go into the bedroom and sit down on the bed.

"Hello," she says with a laugh.

"Happy Easter."

"Happy Easter to you, too. How are things? I know it's been a couple of years since we talked."

"That's right," I say. "I'm good. I was just thinking about you, actually." While not strictly true, it is true that in some sense I'm always thinking of Sandy when I assess my body. Even in our town, where obesity is common, Sandy stood out. "How are you?"

"I'm great," she says. "I work at a little theater in Little Rock."

"Oh, I thought you were in Missouri."

"Well, I landed there for a minute after Gene and I split up, but after a few months I moved here to take this job."

"I see. And you work in a theater? Live theater?"

"Yeah. It's cool. I mostly do office stuff, but they've also let me start dressing sets. You remember that I dabbled in that kind of thing?"

"Of course. You worked on the sets for the Passion Play, didn't you?"

"That's right. I think that doing that stuff was the only thing I really liked about being in the music ministry, in fact."

"Yes. Well, I recall that you did a very nice job. What kind of things do you work on now? What kind of shows?"

"Well . . ." She hesitates. "It's not the kind of thing you'd like, I don't think."

I frown and lean back from the phone. Who is she to assume she knows what I like?

"I like lots of things," I say.

"Oh, I didn't mean it that way. It's just, I don't know if you'd approve. For instance, the latest thing we're working on is an all-drag production of *Oklahoma!* called *Oklahomo!* You think that would be up your alley?"

It takes me off guard, but I laugh a little. "Ah . . . I see your point. Well, I . . . I hope you're having fun, at least."

"I am. I really am. I guess marrying into the ministry wasn't a good idea. That life wasn't a good fit for me."

"I guess not. But you're okay now?"

"I really am. I mean, life ain't perfect, you know, it never is, but I'm in a good place with myself."

"That's nice," I say. "Things are good career-wise, health-wise . . . ?"

She pauses and laughs. "Are you asking if I'm still fat?"

"Well, no, I—"

"Hey, it's okay to ask. My weight was the main thing I thought about from the age of nine to the age of twenty-nine. I certainly know that people at the church talked about it."

"I don't think— I know that everyone always liked you, Sandy."

"Oh, I'm not so sure about that. But I didn't much like myself in those days."

"But now you're good?"

"Yep, now I'm fat and happy. I think changing up my life helped me a lot. New city, new friends, new job, all that. But I also just got to a place with myself where I said, 'Sandy, girl, this is what you look like. You spent twenty years crash-dieting and crying about it. Let's try not giving a shit and see how that works.' Turns out it works great. Hell, I even lost a couple of pounds once I stopped kicking my own ass about it."

I ignore her use of profanity, and I say, "That's great, Sandy. I'm happy to hear it."

She asks about me, and I tell her about each of the children. When I finish, she says, "But you? You're okay?"

"Sure," I say. I'm aware that it comes out halfhearted, but I don't try to compensate for that by saying anything else.

There's a pause, and she says, "Sorry. I didn't mean to pry. I guess we were never really close."

"Well, I'm not really close to anyone," I say. "I guess I always felt I had to hold myself a little apart from people. I hope that doesn't sound cold."

"No. I know what you mean," Sandy says. "Being a preacher's wife is a twenty-four-hour-a-day job."

"Yes. It is. That's exactly right. And I like it. I'm not complaining. But it takes a lot out of you. It's like being a politician's wife. To a lot of people, it barely looks like a job at all, but it's like that thing Ginger Rogers said about dancing with Fred Astaire."

"'I did everything he did but backward and in heels.'"

"Exactly. The ministry is a business of relationships. I have to manage every relationship Richard does, but I have to do it without the imprimatur of being an ordained minister. And I have to always be sweet and nice and all that."

"You have to be a lady."

"Right."

"You literally have to do it in heels."

We both laugh at that. "Exactly."

"How is Fred Astaire?"

"Richard? Oh, you know, he's . . . Richard." And I think of that phone call this morning. And his strange attack at the breakfast table later. At first, I feared it might be a heart attack. Now I've begun to think it looked more like a panic attack. *Did it have something to do with the phone call?*

I shake my head.

"He's out and about today," I say. "I'm not really sure where he is right now . . ."

"Good old Brother Richard," she says. "I never got to know him very well."

"No. No one does."

"I'm surprised to hear you say that," she says. "I always thought of him as the most popular man in Van Buren County."

"Sure," I say, "but he's everyone's confidant and no one's confider."

God, shut up, Penny.

"Lord, listen to me," I say quickly. "I must be in a mood or something today, Sandy."

Sandy seems surprised, but she hurries to laugh and reassure me, "It's okay, Penny."

"Anyway . . . ," I say, trying to sound cheerful.

She clears her throat. "Well, listen, actually the reason I'm calling, besides wanting to catch up with you, is that I was wondering if you knew anything about Clarissa Sullivan. I'm trying to get into contact with her now to see if she'd like to be part of an upcoming show here, but it looks like she left the school. You're the only person I knew to call."

As I'm telling her that I heard that Clarissa moved to Louisiana to marry a man she met over the internet, my voice and demeanor don't change, but I'm secretly mortified to realize that she didn't call to talk to me. Why did I just open up to someone who was only calling to ask about someone else I barely know? What's wrong with me today?

When it comes time to hang up, Sandy tells me, "It was so great catching up with you, Penny."

"Yes," I say.

"I really . . . I have to say, it was really unexpected. You know, I always admired you and wished we could be friends, so it's nice to talk to you and to be able to talk in such an open and honest way."

She thinks she knows me now, but she doesn't know me well enough to know that she's offended me, embarrassed me. "It was nice to hear from you, Sandy." She doesn't need to know it, either. "I'll tell everyone you called. Brother Weatherford will be glad to hear it."

"Okay," she says. "And if you ever get down to Little Rock and want to take in a show, you know where you can get some free tickets."

"I don't get down to Little Rock," I say.

***

Are they happier now? At the time of their divorce, I joined everyone at church in feeling bad about the dissolution of the Loomis marriage. *Isn't it sad that they couldn't work it out?* was the nice iteration of this sentiment, though *Isn't it sad that Sandy couldn't trust the Lord to work it out?* was the harsher way of assessing the same situation.

But what if Sandy's actually happy now? She says she is, but most people say they're happy when they're not. So, who knows? I do know for sure that she was miserable when she lived here. I always felt like that was obvious. And when she left Gene and moved away, although I went along with the prevailing sentiment that she'd been wrong to leave him, I do remember wondering if it wasn't for the best. Now, to all appearances, it seems like it worked out well.

It's odd. The hardest things to reconcile in the ministry aren't the miseries. I've seen enough bad things happen to good people to understand why so much of the Bible is about suffering. We hope for a better world because this one's full of pain. I understand that. It makes sense. What confounds me are all the moments when the world doesn't work according the dictates of our faith. When Sandy left her husband, Gene tried to stop her because he didn't want to break up their marriage. He even asked Richard to help, and Richard went over and tried to talk her out of leaving. He told her it was a sin for them to get divorced, which, of course, it was.

But then, everything worked out. Gene left the ministry, moved to Missouri, became a high school music teacher, and got remarried. He has three kids now, a boy and twin baby girls. At least according to the story he's telling on Facebook, he's got a good life. I suppose I always assumed Sandy was depressed in Missouri somewhere, but now I find that she's fat and happy, designing gay theater productions in Little Rock.

Did she call just to tell me that? Did she want me to know? She said she wanted to ask about Clarissa, but did she really call to tell me that she's not only happy without Gene, she's happy without the rest of us?

The day he went to talk to her, Richard told her she wouldn't be happy outside the church. Yet, as far as I can tell, she is. In fact, as far as I can tell, she and Gene are both happier now.

What the hell does that mean?

Richard should be home already.

I stop at the top of the stairs and listen to the kids talking, laughing, and arguing. Johnny has roped Matthew and Mary into a silly debate about superheroes. He loves to do this, to weigh the authority of his older siblings. If I understand this particular dispute correctly, Johnny and Matthew are arguing that Batman could beat Wonder Woman in a fight because he's better trained. Mary replies that Wonder Woman is an Amazon and has thus been training for thousands of years. When she adds that Wonder Woman is strong enough to punch Batman's heart out, they all laugh.

Mark, sitting by himself in his room, is listening to Elvis sing "Where No One Stands Alone."

I walk downstairs to put Matthew's and Mary's wet clothes in the dryer. When I come out of the washroom, Johnny calls me from the kitchen to ask my opinion in the superhero debate.

I walk to the kitchen where they're gathered. Matthew is about to take the ice cream out of the refrigerator. "I don't have an opinion on superheroes," I say. "But I do have an idea. Why don't you all go up to Sonic and get ice cream?"

"Hm, that's not a bad idea," Matthew says. "The pickings here are pretty slim."

Mary nods. "This is a phenomenal idea. I'm going to see if Mark wants to go."

She runs upstairs, and a moment later, she and Mark come down.

"You coming, Mama?" he asks me.

"No, I think I'll stay here. I want to talk to your father."

The boys all take in this information nonchalantly, but Mary furrows her brow. She doesn't ask if anything is wrong, but she's more sensitive to my moods than her brothers. She just asks, "Would you like us to get you anything at Sonic?"

"No, thank you."

When the kids are gone, I walk through the quiet of my home, listening to the soft padding of my own feet.

I walk upstairs. I look at the clock.

I sit down on the bed to wait for my husband.

EIGHT GARY DOANE

Mom and Dad aren't home when I come in, so I stop in the kitchen and dig through the refrigerator for leftovers. Lasagna. I don't even heat it up. It's good cold. I'm not going to miss much when I get out of this town, but I will miss Dad's lasagna.

I grab a Coke Zero and carry it down the hall to my room and shut the door.

I pop open the Coke and take a sip. Then I put it on my beside table and plop against the wall and look around. The room is the same as it was when I was in high school. Poster of My Chemical Romance. Poster of *The Shining*. Some art I drew back when I thought I wanted to be an artist.

I won't miss this room.

I fork some lasagna in my mouth as I try to really imagine leaving town. I left once before, when I went away to U of A, but it wasn't like leaving forever. I knew I would be back during the summers and for the holidays. But when I leave town this time, I won't be back for a long time. For years. Hell, I may never come back.

The door to the garage opens. Dad calls out, "Gary?" He's got the usual panic in his voice.

The suicide watch is home.

"In my room," I call back. I sip my Coke and wait.

Sure enough, they both come down the hall. Mom says, "Can we come in?"

"Sure."

The door opens, and there they are, my parents, a little worried, a little relieved. I hate the way they look at me. Especially my poor father.

"Hey, bud," he says, coming in. "How's it going?"

"Good."

He stops at the foot of the bed. Mom lingers in the doorway a second, and then she moves in behind him. "Where you been?" Dad asks, trying to be casual.

"Just out."

"Oh. You didn't tell us where you were going."

"I told you yesterday I was probably going to run around this morning."

Mom tries to smile, but it only comes off looking like a pained attempt not to be irritated. "We tried texting and calling you."

"Yeah, sorry. My phone died. I think something's messed up on it. It can't keep a charge."

"Oh," she says. "We got—we got a little worried."

"There's no reason to worry, Mom."

I feel ridiculous saying it. I'm sitting on a bed they bought, in a house they own, eating food they made. Hard to stand up for yourself under these circumstances.

Dad has on khakis and a navy-blue polo shirt. When he sits down on the bed beside me, he looks like an understanding father on a TV show. "We know there's no reason to worry," he says, jostling my foot. "We're not trying to ride you, son, but look at it from our point of view. We get up, you're gone. Then we can't get you on the phone."

"I told you. It was the battery on my phone."

Dad nods understandingly. "Yeah, that's right." He turns back to Mom. "Just a problem with the phone."

Mom stares at me.

"Everything is cool," I tell them. "Can we just, you know, go on about our day?"

Dad says, "Yep. Of course." He looks back at Mom. "Everything is fine here. Right?"

Mom folds her arms and nods.

"You mad, Mom?" I ask.

She shakes her head. "No. Just glad you're okay."

I know that what she's saying is only partially true. She's relieved that I didn't go drive myself off a cliff or something, but it's not true that she's not mad. She's been mad at me since I came back home to live. Dad is the kind of guy who can love you without it costing him anything. He's got an endless amount of love to give, and he's always eager to give you more. Mom isn't that way. She loves you, but she lets you know that it costs her something to do it.

I tell them, "I'm sorry I worried you guys. I was just out and about. Pretty morning."

"Awesome," Dad says, giving my leg a gentle slap. "Hey, don't forget that we're going over to the Beckers' in a bit."

"Right. Do you mind if I don't go to that with you guys?"

Mom says, "But you love the Beckers."

"Well, yeah. They're great. Just, they're your friends. I don't want to be the fifth wheel. The odd man out."

"Oh, you shouldn't look at it that way," Dad says. "We love to have you there, and Janet and Dale—"

"It's okay," Mom says.

Dad looks back at her.

She tells him, "If he doesn't want to hang around with the old folks, you can't blame him." She asks me, "Do you have other plans?"

"I don't know. Might just goof around."

She pats Dad on the shoulder. "Let him goof around. It'll do him some good."

"Okay," Dad says. "Let us know if you change your mind, though. I think Dale is going to make his ribs."

"Okay," I say.

They get up to leave. Dad spies my empty bowl and dirty fork. "Here," he says. "Let me take that for you."

At moments like this, it's easy for me to spiral into feeling bad about myself. Mom and Dad didn't used to treat me like this. They weren't so scared all the time.

That's my fault, but I have to remind myself that I don't need to feel guilty about making them worry. I shouldn't feel guilty about what happened to me.

I didn't choose for it to happen. It happened *to* me, inside of me. People always want to know why. Hey, me, too.

But it's hard not to feel guilty. My parents weren't prepared. I always did well in high school, and I was always ready to get out of this stupid town, so when I got a scholarship to U of A, everybody just assumed that I'd do great. And at first, I did. My grades were okay, I had a good dorm, and I made a few friends. For the first time ever, I even started dating. I went out with two girls that I told Mom and Dad about, and one guy that I didn't. Nothing magical happened with any of them, but it was all pretty nice. Everything in my life was going fine.

I still don't know why it all came undone my junior year. I think about it all the time. All I know is that when the semester started, I couldn't make myself go to class. I'd get up and get dressed and walk over to the building, but then I'd just keep walking. I'd go to the library and sleep. I'd go to the student center and watch TV. I'd go back to my dorm and lay in bed all day. I stopped hanging out with people. I wasn't even drinking or smoking weed. I just watched TV and slept.

Once all my grades were in the toilet, I started getting stern emails from the school. I was in danger of flunking out, so I dragged myself to my advisor's office. He told me that I was in for a hard climb back, that I would have to do at least one additional year, maybe two, in order to graduate. I puked in his trash can.

I just curled up in bed after that and didn't move for two days. I couldn't eat. I pissed and shit myself. My roommate called for help, and finally the school brought in my parents.

So now I'm home. And Dad is worried. And Mom is furious. And I tell myself I shouldn't beat myself up for falling into a depression because it's not my fault.

I worked with a therapist for a while. I told her it all just got to be too much for me. Life. Living. Walking around being a person with a name and an identity. At a certain point, that just became absurd to me. Why do I have a name? A collection of little letters that goes on papers and forms? Why does that define me? Underneath all that crap you're just an animal that breathes and eats and shits and fucks and dies.

Of course, now I'm back here, in the cradle of my identity. This house. This room. These people. They gave me a name, a religion, my whole identity. *Gary Doane.* Two little words that comprise a symbol, a shorthand, and people think they know what it means. Mom and Dad think they know what it means.

The difference is, now they worry. That's the part I do regret. I feel like I was this great kid for them for a long time, until one day I just broke. They don't know how that happened. They're still trying to figure it out. They blame the school, they say, well, maybe it was drugs or liberal professors or bad roommates or some girl. But it was none of that. Like I told the therapist, it was just life. That's the part they won't face because it's too upsetting. It was life that broke me.

Not too long after Mom and Dad pull out of the driveway, Sarabeth texts me, R ur parents gone?

Yes, I text back.

k be there in a sec

I put down the phone and close my eyes. I'll keep them closed until she gets here. She'll come right in, and I won't open my eyes until she's in front of me. She's the only thing I want to see.

NINE SARABETH SIMMONS

He's not the only guy I've ever been with—far from it—but I'm his first anything. It's weird because he's older than me by like four years almost and he went off to college for a while. He's not ugly or anything, either. I can remember him a little, from when I was a freshman and he was a senior. He was smart and kind of shy. I always figured he was gay. Even now, I'm not sure what he is. He never wants to talk about that with me. In a lot of ways, he's the same as he was in high school. Too quiet, too smart for his own good, too sensitive. But he's sweet. And he's good.

He's doing this weird thing where he doesn't want to open his eyes until I'm undressed. I take off all my clothes, and then I pull off his clothes. He giggles. It makes me smile.

I slide up his body, let my tits run over his skin. He lets out a little groan. I don't stop to blow him because he doesn't really like blow jobs. He's the only guy I ever met—in fact, he's the only guy I ever heard of—who doesn't like blow jobs. But I'm not complaining. Most guys watch too much porn, and they can't wait to stick their dick in your face.

Gary's not like that. He wants to have sex all the time, but it's never really nasty with him. He wants to kiss a lot. He wants to look me in the eyes while we do it.

He does. I climb on top of him and put him inside me, and he stares into my eyes. He likes to watch me, and I like him to watch me. Other guys have made me feel horny; some even made me feel nasty. And I liked it, mostly. Everybody wants to be nasty sometimes, I guess. But with Gary, it's different.

He's the only guy I've ever met who actually makes me feel sexy. It washes over me, that feeling of being sexy, of being pretty enough to watch. He's totally into me, but he doesn't seem to want anything from me. He's never in too big a hurry to come, and he doesn't beg me to blow him or let him stick it in my ass. He's just really into me. It's weird, but he makes me feel younger than I am.

"I love you," I say.

He slows down, smiles, brings my face down to his and kisses me. "I love you, too."

We're staring at his blank, white ceiling.

I say, "I have to tell you something."

The way I say it makes him look over at me. "What?"

"I'm starting to get nervous," I say.

"About what?"

"About him. About Holy Shit."

"What about him?"

"I don't know. About what he might do. Desperate people do desperate shit."

"Yeah, and the desperate thing he's going to do is give us thirty grand," Gary says. "You're not getting cold feet, are you? It's too late for that."

"No. It's just, now that we're in this thing, I'm nervous."

"I understand that," he says, "but this thing is illegal now. It's a little late to start getting nervous. You realize that? This isn't just some shit between him and me anymore, or even him and his church. It's not just about a scandal. I mean, people go to jail for what I did this morning. You need to be realistic about what we're doing here."

I have to stop and think about that for a second. I guess it's true. I never really considered how much shit we'd be in if people knew we were trying to blackmail the preacher. I feel kind of guilty now that I never even thought of that. This whole thing was my idea. I should have considered that.

"You said he was scared shitless this morning?"

"Yes. He knows the fix he's in."

"That's right," I say. "He got what he wanted from you, and now he just wants you to go away, right? He's got a wife and twenty-seven thousand kids. He's got too much to lose, man. The church, everyone thinking he's the shit. He'll give you the money. He'll raid the donation plate, the savings account, whatever, and then he'll just be happy to get rid of you."

Gary closes his eyes and nods. "Yes." He smiles. "Twenty-seven thousand kids . . . You're funny."

"How many Weatherford kids are there actually? I forget."

"Five."

"Jesus."

"I know."

"I always thought Matthew was a dick."

"Yeah, me, too," Gary says. "Sometimes I used to see him around campus when we were both at U of A. He basically acted like he didn't know me. He went super preppy once he got there."

"Gross."

"Yeah. And Mark was always . . . Mark. You know. I didn't really know Mary in school. She was about your grade, right?"

"Yeah, but I didn't know her very well. She was popular, played basketball and all that. I mean, I guess she was okay, but I never had much to do with her."

He just nods.

"Jesus," I say, "and then they had two more kids?"

"Yeah. After the first three, Richard and Penny stopped having sex. I mean, for like ten years or something, he told me. Then they had Johnny and Ruth."

I shake my head. "You think they have sex now?"

"I think they had just enough sex to have the kids. When you have five kids, it makes you look like you're always fucking, but that's just for show."

"Because he's gay?"

"Honestly, I don't even know. I mean, he's definitely a closet case, but really I think he hates sex. I think he hates bodies. They gross him out. For him, it's all about masturbation. He wants to watch me jack off, and he wants me to watch him. Fucking weirdo."

I turn over and lay on my side and look at him. His face is narrow, with a little nose and thin lips. I never thought he was cute when I was a kid. I never gave it any thought at all. He was just an older guy at my school.

But when he moved back to town after his breakdown, he used to come into the store a lot. He never bought much. I think he just wanted to get out of the house, get away from his parents.

I've met them a couple of times. Gary gets nervous around them, though, so me and him only get together when they're gone. His dad's a trip. One of those guys who's too nice for his own good—that's where Gary gets it, I guess. His mom's kind of a bitch. Both times I talked to her she kept looking at my clothes. I wasn't wearing anything slutty or anything like that. Just a shirt and some jeans, but she kept looking me up and down like she couldn't believe what a no-class piece of shit her son had brought home.

Gary says that's just her look, but I can tell she doesn't like me. She thinks Gary's just this dropout who moved home and now he's hanging out with the girl who works the register at Pickett's. Of course, once she finds out I got fired, she'll really love me.

"Anyway," Gary says, "we'll be done with him soon. He'll give us the money, and then everything will be fine."

I nod. "And we can leave."

"Yep, and then we can do what we want."

"Where do you want to go first?"

"I thought we'd go down to Austin and see that guy I knew from college, Wally."

"Wally, right. He lives down there now, right?"

"Yeah, he's from there originally."

"Why do you want to see him?" I ask.

Gary shrugs. "Oh, I don't know. No particular reason. Just somebody I know."

"You and him . . . You guys were just friends or . . . ?"

He stares at me a second. "You know, it's not like I've slept with everyone I've ever met."

"I know that."

"He's a friend. That's it. A guy I know."

"Okay, okay."

He asks, "Where do you want to go?"

"We can go to Austin, it's fine."

"But if you had your druthers, where would you want to go?"

"Well, I always wanted to see New Orleans. My mom went there once when she was in her twenties, and she loved it. She always said we'd go together, but of course that never happened. So, fuck it. I'll just go on my own. Which is the whole point, right? We can go anywhere we want. Be anybody we want to be."

He smiles. "That's right."

"Hell yeah. That's why I want to leave. People around here decide who they think you are, and then if you try to do something different, they act like you're the one being the asshole. That's how you know the preacher will come up with the money. Because the bigger they are, the harder they fall. I mean, his secrets would ruin his life."

Something occurs to Gary, and he frowns. "You know, if the truth did come out, I guess the only thing I'd worry about is my parents. It'd embarrass them in front of everyone they know."

"Hey, fuck 'em."

He's staring at me. "Don't say that, Sarabeth. You should care more."

"What do you mean?"

"I mean, this whole thing was your idea. You need to care more about the consequences."

"It wasn't *all* my idea. We talked about it. You're the one who said you thought the preacher was throwing you vibe every time you saw him."

"And you're the one who said if I messed around with him, he'd feel guilty and give me money to go away."

"And you're the one who did."

Gary sits up with his back to the wall. "You look down on me for doing that?"

"No, of course not. You know I don't give a shit."

"That's what I'm saying. You don't give a shit."

"Gary . . ."

"Why don't you care? You're supposed to want me all to yourself. You're not supposed to want to share me with anybody."

I sit up, too. I feel weird just sitting here with my tits hanging out, though, so I grab my bra off the floor. "This is bullshit," I tell him. "I didn't make you do anything with the preacher."

"We're not talking about anyone making me do anything. We're talking about how you could care less if I have to jack off with some old pervert so we can get a little money."

I grab my panties off the end of the bed. "You don't get to do this, Gary. You don't get to do something and then blame me because you did it."

He crosses his arms and stares up at the ceiling. "I just . . ."

"You just what?"

"You really don't care, do you? Is this just about the money for you?"

I'm so fucking tired of people giving me shit. I stand up and start getting dressed.

"What are you doing?" he says.

"What's it look like? I'm leaving."

"Why?"

"Because you're being an asshole."

"No, I'm not."

I pull on my jeans.

"Sarabeth . . ."

"No. You know what? Do what you want." I start pulling on my shoes.

"When he pays you, then good for you. You take the money and go away and live happily ever after by yourself."

"Stop it. Sit down. C'mon . . ."

I stomp out of his room and out to my car. As I'm backing out of the driveway, I can see him at the door, sheet around his waist, with a look on his face like a lost kid at the mall.

I think about stopping, but I just keep going.

Fuck him. Fuck everybody.

TEN RICHARD WEATHERFORD

I'm in my driveway. I've driven home, like a drunkard after a party, and I'm not sure how I've made it here. The last few minutes of my life are a blur.

It's a feeling I've felt before—with Gary. The first time we were together, in this minivan, we were parked in the dark down some skinny trail two counties away. I gave in to my temptation, let him lead me to sin *or did i lead him* and when we had finished, I drove home in a daze. I could not remember the drive at all, the stops and turns I had to make to get back into town, back into my neighborhood, back to my home. But there I was, a man sitting behind the steering wheel, staring at his own hands.

And here I am, once again, unsure of just who I am.

I'm Richard Howard Weatherford. I'm the husband of Penelope. The father of Matthew, Mark, Mary, Johnny, and Ruth. I'm the pastor of the First Baptist Church of Stock, Arkansas. I am a Christian. I am a man of God.

What I'm not is a homosexual. There's really no such thing as a homosexual. The concept of gay identity is one of the devil's lies, predicated on the fallacy that homosexuality is a state of being. If homosexuals exist, then God must have created homosexuals; so, no, there can be no homosexuals. There are only homosexual acts, and one can choose whether or not to perform those acts. I can turn away from my sin.

But first I must do this. I must protect my family, my friends, my church.

I look out the windshield of my minivan at my sunny two-story home. I think of all the people who drive by this house and say, "That's where the preacher lives." Something in the weight of all these possessions makes me feel tethered. A car, a home, a small piece of land. A family. A life.

And yet, it all feels so terribly fragile today.

I don't know what Harten will do, how he'll get the money. He carries himself like a desperate man, like he could break a window at any moment to steal food. Being around him makes me nervous; it sent me home as dizzy as if I'd just stepped up to the edge of a cliff.

Please God, I pray, *help him get the money.*

It's an absurdity and a heresy to ask the Lord for assistance in something so low and tawdry as this, of course, but I can't help myself. It's a profane prayer from a profane soul.

I walk inside and the house is curiously quiet. Only now do I realize that I didn't see Matthew's car in the driveway.

"Hello," I call.

My voice seems leaden in the empty house.

"Anyone home?"

"Hey," Penny says from upstairs.

I walk to the bottom of the stairs. "Where is everyone?"

"Come upstairs if you want to talk."

"I said, 'Where is everyone?'"

"And I said to come upstairs if you want to talk."

I climb the stairs and find her sitting on our bed, her back against the wall, feet crossed at the ankles, hands folded on a pillow. I notice that she's taken out her contacts and put on her glasses.

"What are you doing?" I ask.

"Sitting. What are you doing?"

I open my palms as if to show her nothingness itself. "Just got home. Where is everyone?"

"I suggested they go to Sonic for ice cream."

"Oh."

"I thought it would be nice for them all to go together. They never do anything as a group, all of them together."

"Ruth isn't with them."

She nods and stares at me. "I know."

I tell her, "If you wanted Ruth to go with them, you could have told her to stay home."

"I don't care about that."

"Oh. Are you okay?"

"Why do you ask?"

"You're acting weird."

"Am I?" she says.

"Yes."

"How?"

"You're asking me a series of stupid questions, for one thing. You only do that when you want me to guess what's bothering you."

She lowers her chin a bit and stares at me over her glasses, which is something she does when she wants to take me to task. "And what would your guess be?"

"I haven't the faintest clue."

"You haven't the faintest clue."

"No. I do not. So why don't you stop prevaricating and tell me what's wrong."

She unfolds her hands and looks out the window. She's not really looking out the window, though. Not really. She's making me stare at her and wait. Such dramatics.

Finally, she says, "Why don't you sit down?"

I make a show of walking to the bed and sitting down a few inches from her feet. "Yes?" I say.

"Where have you been all day?"

"What?"

"Where have you been all day?"

"I haven't . . . I've been here. I went out to see Terry Baltimore this morning. I came home, had breakfast with the family, had a nap, talked to Randy, then I took Ruth over to Scarlett's house. Then I came home. All of which you already know, so what are you doing? Why would you ask me where I've been?"

She pulls her arms tighter to her torso and stares at the bedspread.

"That's right," she says. "I know all that."

"Then what's wrong?"

"You've been somewhere else."

"What do you mean?"

"You haven't been here with us."

"You mean . . . Oh, you mean I've been distracted?"

She tries to smooth a wrinkle in the bedspread as she says, "Sure."

"Well, I have a lot on my mind. I've been thinking about a lot of things, you know. This dry vote coming up. I've been giving that a lot of thought. Been thinking really hard about that. And then the Passion Play tomorrow. I still need to go up to the church today."

"Yes. Of course."

I reach over and pat her leg. "I'm sorry if I've been distant. I don't mean to be."

She looks up at me, and there are tears in her eyes. I begin to move toward her, but she holds out a hand. "You just stay . . . just stay right over there."

"Penny, what on earth is wrong with you? Is this some kind of woman thing?"

Her skin changes color. She swings her legs to the floor, the pillow tumbles off her lap, and she slaps my face.

I grab her arms and shove her back onto the bed.

"What are you doing?" I demand, standing over her. "Have you lost your mind?"

"Maybe I just found it."

"What does that mean?" I step across the room and shut our bedroom door. "What does that mean? Answer me."

Her face is flushed, her eyes full of furious tears. I haven't seen her this angry in years. Perhaps I've never seen her this angry. We've never come to blows before, not even in our worst times.

She shakes her head, puts her hands over her ears.

She says, "I don't think . . . I don't think I love you."

My own ears are ringing. It's not from the slap, though. All I can find to say is, "What?"

Staring at me, her eyes grow wide as if they're hungry to take in more light. She drops her hands to her lap. "I don't. I don't love you. Maybe I never did."

"That's ridiculous. If—"

"Just shut up, Richard, and listen to me. When we met, you were looking for a Christian wife, and I was looking for a Christian husband. That's why we got married. That's what our attraction was based on from the very beginning. Do you know I never fantasized about you?" She reads something on my face and responds to it. "Romantic nonsense, right? The kind of thing that you mock from the pulpit. You don't believe in that kind of thing. You only believe in God's will. You *say*. You *say* you only believe in God's will, but have you ever noticed how God's will and your will always seem to be aligned?"

"We're supposed to align ourselves to God's will, Penny."

"And God tells you what his will is, and then you tell the rest of us."

"That's a little simplistic, Penny, but yes, roughly speaking, the Lord instructs me, and I instruct others. It's the way it's always been. I thought it was the way you liked it. You're acting like I'm some self-serving jerk, but forgive me for pointing out that you've always relished the role of queen bee of the church. With your Ladies' Auxiliary and your little meetings."

"My little meetings," she says.

"You know what I mean."

"Oh," she says, "I know what you mean better than you do."

"Of course you do."

"Well, I do."

"By all means, explain it to me. That's what you do. The feminists accuse men of 'mansplaining,' but what about womansplaining? That's when a woman tells a man what he *really* meant."

"That's cute, Richard. I bet you've been working on that for a while now."

The truth is, I have. I was going to use it as a joke in a sermon. Comparing her to feminists is a cheap shot. I do it to hurt her, to enrage her. I'm not sure why, though. I should be trying to dial down this fight rather than exacerbate it. Maybe it's because she hit me and my face still stings. If I can't hit her back, at least I can infuriate her.

She says, "You know I'm not a feminist, you idiot."

"Name calling. Excellent. First you hit me. Then you say you don't love me. Then you start calling me names."

She crosses her arms and shakes her head, too disgusted to look at me.

I ask, "So what is the problem exactly? What am I lacking? Explain it to me."

"You have no compassion, Richard. You don't really believe in it. You think it would weaken you somehow."

"What are you talking about? I work hard for people. I visit the sick and elderly. I help people in times of crisis. I think all those folks would be shocked to hear that I don't believe in compassion."

"No, you believe in duty. You help people because you think you're supposed to. Like a garbage collector picking up the trash. You're a man doing a job. There's no real compassion in you, no empathy."

"Wow. I sound like a really awful person, Penny. Thank you for enlightening me."

She breathes through her nose. She closes her eyes. She says, "You don't care about me, Richard."

"And now I don't care about you."

"It's not a new thing. It's an old thing. Like I said, we got married because we thought it made sense. We had children because we thought it made sense."

"So, is that what this is? You're rethinking our marriage now?"

She rubs her nose. "I've rethought our marriage so many times." She looks up at me. Her face has returned to its natural color. Her eyes are still a little pink, but they're not full of tears anymore. "When I was young, I tried to be the wife you wanted me to be. When that didn't work, I tried to make you the husband I wanted you to be. That didn't work, either. So in the end, I guess I settled for raising the children the way I thought they should be raised, in a good home, in a good church."

"We brought them up right."

"We? Yes. You're their father, and they love you."

"Oh, well, thank you for granting me that, at least. I'm relieved to hear that my children love me."

"Sometimes, I wish they didn't."

"Penny . . ."

"You let them come to you. You let them love you. You let them compete for your attention. And it works. They all love you, and they all want you to love them, to forgive them for the many sins you see in them."

That stops me. "Now you're just being ugly," I say. "Now you're just being cruel."

"I'm being honest," she says. "It's the same thing as being cruel sometimes."

The way she says it makes me sick. The grandiosity, the sense of superiority. "Thank you for your honesty," I say. "What do you want to do, get a divorce?"

I intend these words as a jab, but in one terrible instant I am aware that part of me hopes she'll answer yes.

"Of course not," she says, and when she says it, I'm filled with an even more terrible sense of relief. "Too many people believe in us. It's not like Sandy and Gene. No one lost their faith because the Loomises got divorced. But there are too many people who need us to keep being Brother and Sister Weatherford. We don't just have our children to think about; we have our church, the whole town in some ways . . . That's the truly awful part." She stops and shakes her head. "We're too big to fail."

"Then what do you want?" I ask.

She sighs. "For you to be honest."

"I am honest."

"Are you? We've been together a long time, Richard. I've given you a houseful of children so you could feel like a man. I've let you make fun of me in sermons so you could look like some kind of guy's guy. I've toed the party line. And I'm not going anywhere. I'll bury you, or you'll bury me. One way or the other. But don't stand there and tell me you went and saw Terry Baltimore this morning."

I stare at her.

Downstairs, the front door opens and the children come in, laughing and loud, Johnny already seeking us out.

"The kids are home," I say.

She shakes her head. "That's it? 'The kids are home.' You're going to hide behind the children?"

"I have to go to church. It's almost two, you know. I have Easter practice with the choir and the actors."

She rubs her face with both hands, checking for tears. "Two. Right. You need to go."

"And you, you have things to do up at the church this afternoon, right?"

"Yes, one of my little meetings."

"Penny . . . My point is, we can talk about this later."

She stands up and crosses the room. "Of course."

I almost reach out for her, but I know that's not what she wants. Instead, I step away from the door and tell her, "I love you, Penelope."

Her hand on the doorknob, she closes her eyes. "Do you know you haven't told me that in years?" she says.

"It's true, though. I do."

She looks back at me with nothing eyes, and she nods, but I'm not sure exactly what she's nodding at.

Then she opens the door and walks downstairs to our children.

PART TWO SATURDAY EVENING

ELEVEN BRIAN HARTEN

I'm sitting in Roxie's car just up the road when the collector passes me on his way to Tommy's Bar. His name is Frankie James. He has a brother named Jesse. Of course he does. His parents are fucking idiots. Frankie's not really an idiot, though. He's a pretty sharp guy. I need to keep that in mind while I try to get away with this.

It's about five, so he's probably just coming in. This is about the time I used to get to work. Tommy will line Frankie out on some stuff, and then he'll give him his marching orders for the night. Then Tommy will go home for a while and Frankie will take off to make the daily collections. I don't know what route he'll take, but he'll have to hit at least three places around town: Tommy's Other Bar, Tommy's Car Wash, and Tommy's Slices. Tommy also has a piece of Arkansas Integrity Lumber, but I don't know if Frankie will do a collection there or not. When I was doing the collecting, I only collected from the lumberyard once in a blue moon. Most of the time, Tommy works out his cut with Hank Dobson over there and Hank cuts him a check.

Everything else, though—the two bars, the pizza place, and the car wash—all operate on a cash-only basis. Frankie will make the collections, and then he'll bring them back here. Tommy will come in later to do his creative accounting.

I could follow Frankie, maybe jump him going back out to his car after his last collection and then knock him on the head, but that's too risky. This ain't the movies. I'm pretty sure if you hit a guy on the head, all you'll do is hurt his head. Wearing a mask wouldn't help, either, because Frankie knows me.

Nope, I need to make a distraction up front, get everyone out there, then sneak in the back and grab the cash.

Saturday night about six or seven o'clock is when the most money is in the cash office. Tommy always folds over Friday into Saturday. So, the cash office should have the Friday take from both bars, plus today's take from the pizza place and the car wash. Put that all together, and I should have enough to pay off the preacher.

Maybe.

The parking lot is starting to fill up.

My cell phone buzzes. Roxie. I let it go to the messages.

I fire up Roxie's car and pull away.

I head over to Walmart to buy a gas can. One of the first jobs I ever had was working here. Hated it. Pushed carts. There's a shit job for you. Of course, now they have a little machine that pushes the carts. They send out one guy with the machine, and he can clean the whole damn parking lot in ten minutes without breaking a sweat. Back in my day, though, they worked us like mules. They kept two of us out there sizzling on the asphalt for the whole eight-hour shift. It was even worse in the winter, breaking your back wrangling ten or fifteen carts in the snow, freezing your balls off while the manager stood in the doorway with his arms crossed. There was no getting ahead, either. In the time it took you to corral ten carts from a parking lot the size of a football field, twenty people had already walked through the front door.

Story of my goddamn life.

I walk in, and the place is as busy as ever. I wave to the girl at the Customer Service desk. I forget her name, but she comes into Tommy's Bar a lot. I should remember her damn name, but I can't. We never really talked.

"Hey, Brian," she says.

I keep going, but I stop after a few steps.

She knows my name. Of course she does. Every third person here knows me. Everyone's going to remember seeing me.

Shit.

I spin around and hurry back toward the door. The girl behind the counter says, "Well, that didn't take long."

"Forgot my wallet," I say, and keep walking.

―――――

Roxie calls again. I shut off the phone.

I stop at a Citgo and buy a two-liter of Mountain Dew. Then I get out of Morrilton and drive for a while just to put some space between me and town. Don't want to make conversation with anybody I know. Once I'm out where there's nothing but blacktop and trees, I swing over the side of the road and empty the bottle in the grass.

I drive all the way over to Birdtown, to a single-pump gas station out in the middle of nowhere. The station itself is just a clapboard shack run by a little old lady who's been sitting behind the register since they discovered gas.

I go inside to pay. The old lady's got a horse face, and she gives me a creaky smile with a mess of long, skinny teeth.

"Howdy."

"Howdy." I hand her five bucks. "Five."

"Boy," she says, "five dollars sure don't get you much these days."

"Nope."

"First gallon of gas I ever sold cost fifty-eight cents. You believe that?"

"Hard to imagine now, ain't it?"

"Sure is."

"All right, now, you have a good one."

"You, too."

I walk out to the pump, but I keep an eye on the old lady through the front window. She's not paying me much mind. She's gone back to staring at the cigarettes and candy.

I unholster the gas nozzle and pull out the plastic bottle, but then I realize the goddamn spout on the bottle is too small. Gas will go everywhere.

I pull out my pocket knife and cut the neck off the plastic bottle. Then I slip the nozzle into the new hole and pull the trigger and gas shoots in, filling it up double quick. It overflows on my hands.

God-fucking-damnit.

I stick the nozzle in the car and put in the rest of my five bucks. Roxie is going to give me hell, so much hell, for keeping her car out like this. Be lucky if she doesn't call the cops on me. Wouldn't that be the shit? She calls the cops and they pull me over while I've driving around with half a Molotov cocktail in the front seat.

I get in, balance the jug between my knees, but the fucking thing slops all over me before I can get it situated.

Pull out of the lot. Slow. My crotch smells like gas. Christ.

Just down the road, I pull over, open the door, dump out half the gas. I don't need the whole damn jug. Just need enough.

Back at Tommy's Bar, I don't see Frankie's car or Tommy's truck, so I drive on by and pull off the road behind a rotted-out barn to wait.

Not sure why they don't knock down these old barns. All over this state, there are barns rotting on the side of the road. Warped gray boards and rusted tin roofs. Depressing. Barn like this, I always think about the farmer who used to own it, twenty, thirty years ago. Hell, maybe more. Maybe back in the Great Depression. At any rate, it was somebody's dream at some point. Out here working his ass off. Then what happened? Ran out of cash, maybe. Or the bankers fucked him. Or maybe he just got old and died.

Now, there's a depressing thought. Either he was a failure and his barn is rotting on the side of the road, or he was a success and his barn is rotting on the side of the road.

Cars keep pulling into Tommy's parking lot. It's what? A little after six now. He does good business. Always has.

I punch the dashboard. What kind of sense does it make that a fucker like Tommy—a guy who's nothing special on his best day—gets to have everything fall into place for him? In high school, the dumb fuck never opened a book. It's not like he studied or worked hard. Even with baseball, he never really trained. I mean, not any more than anyone else. He's just one of those guys who seems to catch every green light.

Well, not tonight, Tommy.

I can see Frankie pull into the parking lot. He gets out of his car with a limp backpack over one shoulder. The backpack is mostly empty, but at the bottom of it, I know, is a little pile of money.

It won't get dark soon enough. I'll have to go down there while it's still light out.

There's an old Walmart bag mixed in with the garbage on Roxie's floorboards. I stuff it in my pocket. I grab the bottle and get out and stand there by the car. Look around. Nothing but trees and dirt. I take off through the trees. My heart is beating so bad my ears start ringing. I take some deep breaths, keep moving.

No choice at this point. No option. This is what's going to happen.

Behind Tommy's, the ground slopes, so I go down into a little damp gully back there and watch things. The back door is propped open like usual to help ventilate the kitchen. Tommy's got a couple of Mexicans back there doing nothing but dropping onion rings and tater tots into crackling grease for hours on end, and the kitchen gets hotter than hell.

I creep down the gully and take a look at the front parking lot. Maybe seven or eight cars, which is pretty normal this early in the evening. No smokers outside. No one by their cars.

I take a deep breath and hurry up the hill, keeping one eye on the door.

I pour the gas on the legs of the statue, splash some up on Tommy's fake bronze balls. Then I take out my lighter and fire it up.

I scorch my hand, but then the statue goes up in flames. Just like that, like the thing is fucking Burning Man.

I take off running to the woods, and I'm almost to the trees before I remember that my crotch is soaked in gasoline. I duck behind a tree and check myself. Luckily, no fire in my pants.

Black smoke is coming off Tommy's statue now, drifting out over the trees. I ditch the bottle and start creeping back up the gully when I hear the front door of the bar open. Someone yells. Once I'm out of eyeshot of the front door, I run up the hill to the side of the building. Inside, there's a ruckus, chairs scraping against the floor, yelling, cussing. I keep low by the windows as I run around to the back door and peek inside. I can see up the hall, through the window on the Employees Only door, across the bar, and to the front. Everyone is heading outside.

I'm through the back door to Tommy's office door. It's locked, but I unlock it with my spare key. I shouldn't have a spare, of course, but I do. I guess that makes me a bad person.

The office is empty. Cash on the desk. Cash in the open safe. Backpack on one chair.

I sweep the cash off the desk into my bag. Then I run over to the safe, pull out all I can, and throw it in the bag.

Then I'm to the door. I crack it. Down the hall, someone runs out of the janitor's closet slopping water as they hustle the mop bucket to the front.

I'm out the back. Across the empty back lot. Up the hill. Through the woods.

I'm running so hard my lungs are on fire. I can smell the smoke from here, can hear the yelling. I look back, but I can't see anything through the trees. Which is a good thing. If I can't see them, it means they probably can't see me. Frankie James won't stand out there cussing at Tommy's burning statue for too long before he thinks to go check on the money he left in the office.

I get to the road, see the old barn. I make sure no one is coming and dash across the blacktop and jump in the car.

I don't tear out, though. I ease out, heading down the road, away from the bar, like a man out for a drive.

TWELVE RICHARD WEATHERFORD

As we're wrapping up the run through of the Passion Play, Mabel Lardner approaches me and draws my attention to the cross, where Cody Crawford is taking a selfie.

We've been doing the Passion Play for as long as I've been pastor of this church, and in every production, Cody has portrayed the Lord because he's the only man in the congregation with long hair and a beard. Despite having been divorced, Cody's the natural casting choice, and as a result, I have ignored occasional whispers about his drinking. He's a good man and a faithful member of the flock, and since he's willing to put on a loincloth and climb up on the cross every Easter, I try to cut him some slack.

But I can't have him taking a selfie.

Mabel asks me, "Is that boy up there taking a photograph of himself?" She's a squat, onion-shaped old woman, clutching her hands together in front of her as if she's afraid she'll split apart.

"I think he might be," I say.

"I don't think that's proper, do you?"

"I'll go talk to him."

"I doubt our Lord felt photogenic at Calvary," Mabel notes helpfully. "Perhaps you should tell Cody to consider that."

"I . . . will. Thank you, Miss Mabel."

As I'm walking over to Cody, Penny passes through the sanctuary with a couple of her Ladies' Auxiliary acolytes in tow. She's dispensing final orders about the proper cleaning of the Easter costumes. She sees me but says nothing.

I wave at Cody. "Hey, Cody."

"Hey, Preacher," he says. "We done?"

"Yeah. Good job. Thanks so much for playing the Lord again this year."

"Heck, I'm just happy I can help out."

Dripping fake blood and real sweat, he climbs down from the cross. He's put on a few pounds since last Easter, and he's sporting a bit of a belly. I may have to talk to him about that next year, maybe ask him to diet. I don't relish that conversation.

The ladies are packing up their purses and notebooks and music sheets, and I speak softly so that they might not hear what I'm saying.

"Cody, can I ask you, were you taking a selfie just now?"

He smiles and nods and pulls the cell phone out of his loincloth. "Yeah, I posted it to Facebook."

"Yeah . . . the thing is, I wish you wouldn't."

"Oh. Really?"

"Yeah, I just don't think it would be appropriate to have a selfie of you dressed as our Lord and Savior. It might be seen as rather flippant."

He stares at me, obviously disappointed but also a little insulted. "I didn't mean nothing by it."

"Of course not, of course not, but intent isn't really the issue. There are things we don't intend to do, pain we don't intend to cause, but if people take it that way, then our intentions don't really matter, because the damage is already done. See what I mean?"

He looks over my shoulder at Mabel Lardner, who is lingering in her pew trying to look casual. Tipping back his crown of thorns and scratching his head, he asks, "That old woman rat me out?"

"She . . . expressed concern about the selfie."

He crosses his arms, smearing fake blood across his bare chest. "She don't even know the word *selfie*," he says.

"C'mon now, brother, that's no way to be. You can see that she's got a bit of a point. So will you, for me, please take down the photo?"

"Oh, Brother Weatherford," Penny calls across the sanctuary. "We're all done here. Everything is in place, so I'm headed home." She says this for the benefit of everyone else in the sanctuary, imbuing *Oh, Brother Weatherford* with a touch of playful humor. This makes Mabel and the other ladies smile.

I smile back. "Okay, honey," I tell Penny. "I'll be home soon." I wave at the others. "Thank you, ladies."

Everyone is saying their good nights, and when I turn back to Cody, I say, "So, are we good here?"

He shrugs and opens the pictures on his phone and deletes the image. "Okay," he says. "Don't want to offend nobody."

"I really do appreciate it," I say.

"Sure. No problem."

I watch as he wraps himself in a white sheet and heads to the baptismal dressing room to change. Mabel smiles at me and, satisfied, collects her purse and Bible to go home.

I shake my head. *What a ridiculous job this is.*

Penny and the ladies have left now, and the church is silent. I wander through the hallway downstairs, checking to see that the doors are locked and the lights have all been turned off. My shoes scratch against the carpet, my breathing is heavy, but the classrooms are empty, and the fellowship hall is quiet and dark. I walk upstairs to the sanctuary.

I've always loved being here by myself. When other people are here, I'm always thinking about them, thinking about the sermon I'm preaching, but when I'm here alone I can relax in a way I can't really relax anywhere else. We don't have actual stained-glass windows, just plastic overlays on the glass, but the pale blue light of the sanctuary is just as soothing as if the windows were real.

Two carpeted aisles divide the pews into three sections. Almost every Sunday, these pews are filled. Three hundred people, on average, come here every week to hear me deliver a message from God. They sit in these seats, facing me quietly, as I slowly pace the stage above them, Bible in hand, telling them what God wants them to do with their lives.

Not all of them buy it, of course. Some look at me with veiled skepticism, more than a few look bored—look bored no matter what I say or how I say it. But most of them do believe me. I can see it on their faces. Almost all of them want me to reassure them, to tell them that the world's insanity has a spiritual context, that no matter what is happening to them—cancer, abuse, depression, debt—that God has a plan, that everything will eventually make sense.

Yes, the job is ridiculous sometimes, but I do some good work here.

I sit down at the edge of the stage and stare at the vacant pews.

I built this congregation. Of course, the church itself has been here for over seventy years, but before I got here, attendance had never risen above a hundred and fifty. I took a congregation the last pastor had merely been babysitting, and I built on it, person by person. I grew the attendance to almost four hundred with nowhere to go but up.

Then, a few years ago, things stalled. I don't know why. We'd had the usual political tussles and petty power struggles, the kind of family squabbles you find in any church, but there was no great scandal. The largest fight had occurred when I tried to step out on faith and build a bigger sanctuary for the expanding congregation, and a vocal minority in the church—led, of course, by Brother Amos—opposed the plan. Amos fought me tooth and nail. I never really understood why, except that perhaps this leaky old building meant more to him than my ministry and the will of God. He was able to get a majority of the deacons on his side, and together they voted down my plans.

Maybe that defeat broke my momentum, or maybe I simply peaked. Maybe old Amos was right, after all. I was never going to have the megachurch I sometimes saw in my dreams at night.

Now, with nearly three hundred souls in attendance every week, I still have the biggest congregation in the county, but it's a soft number. If I'm honest, I have to admit that I've become the kind of preacher that I always detested. I'm just another spiritual babysitter.

It wasn't what I had planned, this life I'm living. I never wanted to mark time in a place like Stock. The name itself is so old and small, with the lingering stink of Ozark backwater to it. I wanted to be the next Rick Warren. I wanted to do great things for God, if only God had chosen me to do great things.

But this place is too small, and the people are, too. They don't come here to be inspired. They don't come here to be motivated to go out and win the world for Christ. They come here to be coddled, to be told that the world outside the limits of our little town is a world gone mad, that they're better off staying here. They huddle in this church as if in a besieged fort while I confirm their prejudices and give them a weekly dose of reassurance that everything's going to work out for those of us who have God on our side. Then we all go home and watch television.

A leader is only as good as his followers. This is what they want, so this is what they get.

Such bitterness. Perhaps this is what Penny sees when she looks at me.

I bow my head to pray.

But what about you, Lord? I haven't spoken to you at length in quite a while. Not really. I've gone through my daily and weekly rituals for the benefit of my family and my congregation. But when was the last time I talked to you?

O Heavenly Father, what can I confess to you that you don't already know? I know there are no secrets kept from you, only truths that men hide from each other. And so I know I should confess, not for your sake, but for mine.

Should I confess my darkest secret to you, Lord? It's not my sinful dalliance with Gary. Nor is it the solicitation of a bribe from Brian.

No, my darkest secret, the one that I've kept hidden even from myself, is that I don't know if you're really there.

Have I ever felt your presence? I've begun to doubt.

Am I only living this life because I know how to be Richard Weatherford, the preacher of this church? Maybe. I certainly don't know how to be anyone else. Could the truth be so terrifyingly simple? That I have nowhere else to go and no one else to be?

I've always considered my vocation a calling. I suppose that all clergymen fancy themselves descended from the priests of old, those prophets with dust on their feet and blood on their hands, leading their people through the deserts with nothing but promises. I've enjoyed seeing myself that way for years now.

People call me Brother or Reverend or Pastor or Preacher. The word I like is Preacher. A gruff word, an American word, a utilitarian word.

What is a preacher, though? A preacher plays many different roles in many different lives, whatever the situation requires. A carnival barker, a marriage counselor, a businessman, a con man, a philosopher, a medium, a magician. Maybe a preacher is just an actor playing the part of a preacher. Maybe you didn't choose me for anything. Maybe I chose myself because I wanted to be onstage.

I've played my part well. But beyond my performance, what is real? I preach salvation, but the truth is that I see very little worth saving. I proclaim miracles, but I only see biology, physics, and coincidence misinterpreted through the lens of ignorance and superstition. I preach your love, but sometimes the only thing that seems more outlandish than your existence is the idea that you love us.

Could it all, in the end, mean nothing? Would that be better?

After a time, I lift myself from the stage and stumble out of the sanctuary and down the hallway to my office. I pass the prayer room, the bathrooms, the youth minister's office. I lock the door to my office and sit down at my desk.

I am left, as we all are, with the world as it is.

What can I do with this disaster I've created?

I could go with him.

The thought itself causes a change in my body. My hands and face dampen. I feel a drop of sweat fall through my chest hair.

If Gary would have me, I could just leave town with him.

Imagine leaving behind this . . . this pettiness, this smallness. The squabbles over nothing, the endless casserole dinners, the forced conversations I have with people who have never read a book, the same people who lie to my face about their sex lives and their alcohol consumption. To never have to preach another funeral, to never have to stand over another tiny casket while a young mother sobs in anguish. And, God, to never have to preach another wedding . . .

The notion of leaving all this behind sends a shiver up my back, pimples the skin on my neck and arms.

But just as quickly, my body readjusts itself. I lean back in my chair, in my office, in my church, just a few miles away from where my family waits for me in my home.

I'm scared and I'm tired, so it only makes sense that I would entertain the notion of running away. Even Christ had his moment in the garden.

Maybe I don't love my life the way I once did. Maybe I've been lying to myself now for years. But where else could I go? Who else could I be?

Not a gay man. Never that. This sin of mine is just that—a sin, a weakness. It's not an identity. I would rather die at this desk and be remembered as a holy man than live a life defined by a sin.

And I can't imagine a life without my children. Penny may think I love them imperfectly—*doesn't every father?*—but they are my world, and my dreams are largely dreams of them. I think of Matthew running for office. I think of giving Mary away on her wedding day. I think of Mark struggling to find his path through this world. I think of the grandchildren that, soon, my children will give to me. And to Penny. Penny, who knows me, in so many ways, better than anyone.

The name of Richard Weatherford means something to the three hundred people of this congregation. It means something to my children. And if there is a God in heaven, then my name must mean something to him.

If there is no God in heaven, if I'm truly alone, then my name is all I have.

I will not give it up without a fight.

THIRTEEN SARABETH SIMMONS

I'm standing in the doorway of Tommy's Bar, holding a beer and watching the smoke puffing off the wet glob of shit that used to be his stupid statue, when Frankie James walks up and says, "You better get out of here."

"Why?" I ask. "I want to see his face when he sees it."

Frankie's got shaggy black hair and a stubbly gray beard, and all of it is sweaty. He wipes his face off with a faded old handkerchief and says, "Somebody called the cops. If they get here, and you're in here drinking underage . . ."

"Shit."

I put down my beer and head on out to my car. Before I leave, I tell the closest waitress, "Don't call Tommy yet. Let me tell him."

I'm racing back to the house all excited because I get to tell Tommy that his goofy statue burnt down—I always thought it was *so* dumb for a guy to have a statue of himself—but I don't get too far down the road before I start thinking about Gary again.

Fuck. I can't get away from him.

The thing is, I know he's right. I guess I did shove him toward the preacher. Maybe I shouldn't have done that. At the time, it seemed smart. Gary said he thought Weatherford was a closet case. I thought, *Well, hell, if he's throwing Gary a vibe, then Gary should fuck him or jack him off or whatever, and then we can get some money out of him.* I mean, it wasn't about Gary. It was about Weatherford.

My mind. I'm always thinking. I must be a real dumb-ass to have done all the thinking I've done and to wind up where I am.

What a goddamn idiot.

If I'm honest, I got to say that no guy ever treated me better than Gary. I mean, he's been real sweet to me. He's a sweet person.

So, did I push this sweetheart of a guy into fucking around with the preacher?

I guess I did. I mean, I didn't make him do it. And I didn't make him half a fag. I guess God did that, if you believe in that sort of thing. Hell, maybe we're all half a fag. I never kissed a girl, but I guess if you stranded me on a desert island with a girl, I bet we'd end up fucking.

Gary doesn't like to talk about it, though. Not just about what he did with Weatherford, either. I can't even really get him to tell me about what happened when he was in college. I'm not sure if there was another boy or what. In a way, I don't really see what the big deal is. I mean, people on the internet and TV can be gay, and nobody cares. In New York and LA and places like that, nobody cares. Hell, I heard they have gay clubs in Little Rock and Eureka Springs. It's 2016. Half the world totally doesn't give a shit.

I come up over a hill and pass a little Church of Christ with one of those signs with the replaceable plastic letters. The message this week reads: A NO TO JESUS IS A YES TO HELL.

Right. This ain't New York or LA or Little Rock. It ain't even Eureka Springs. This is the other half of the world. Me and Gary grew up in Stock, and in Stock being gay is still a sin. And not one of those little sins, like cussing or whatever. Outside of molesting kids or killing somebody, it's about the worst thing you can do. I heard that my whole life, and my heathen ass wasn't even brought up in the church.

Gary was, though. More than me, anyway.

That's exactly why I told Gary that if he thought the preacher was giving him the eye, we should turn it into money. If Gary is gay—if that's the right word for it . . .

So are you gay? I asked. *I don't know exactly,* he said. *You know I don't care,* I said. *I'm just asking.* He said, *I guess I'm queer, or maybe just 'questioning,' as they say. I just really don't know. I mean, I find a lot of men sexually attractive. But I also find most them kind of personally . . . repulsive? Hey*—I laughed—*if finding men sexually attractive and personally repulsive makes you queer, then maybe that's what I am.*

Whatever name you want to put on it, it was the church that taught Gary to hate himself for being who he is. So, yeah, fuck that preacher.

I never liked Brother Weatherford, not since I was in junior high. He'd only been here a couple of years when he went on this big crusade against secular music. I think he heard that Katy Perry song about kissing a girl. A bunch of the fucking Baptist kids at school threw away their old CDs and tapes, even some vinyl. I remember they burned it all in a barrel out behind the church. That pissed me off. And the funny thing was, I don't know if anybody even had that Katy Perry CD. I mean, who the fuck buys CDs anymore? I've never bought music in my life. So most of what they threw away was shitty and old—I think a lot of Spice Girls and Backstreet Boys went down in flames that day—but still, it was like a flashback to the nineties. And then, the kicker was, after a while, he just forgot about it. It's not like they're still out there burning old albums and stuff. He just moved on. His new thing is to stop Brian Harten from opening a liquor store. It's so stupid. Like half the people in Stock ain't alcoholics. They just have to drive twenty minutes to Center Ridge to get their booze.

So, Gary got involved with him. Is that my fault?

Maybe a little.

I look at my phone. He texted me after I ran out on him, but then he let it go quiet when I didn't respond. He's been waiting for me.

I text him, Meet me at my house.

After only a couple of seconds, he texts back, Okay.

When I pull up to the house, I can see that Momma ain't home, but Tommy is. When I come in, he's sitting in his recliner wearing a pink polo shirt and cargo shorts. Trump is on TV calling somebody an asshole. Tommy mutes it as I'm closing the front door.

Before I can say a word about the statue, he says, "Heard you got fired."

"What?"

"That true?"

"Why don't you mind your own business? You *should be* worried about your own business."

I walk down the hall to my room and shut the door. I can hear him clomping right behind me. He just opens my door like it's his.

"What the fuck, Tommy? This is my room; you can't just barge in here."

He's standing there, gut pressed against his shirt, and he's got this dumb look on his face. "My house, my door, my room."

"Yeah, well, you can have it."

He crosses his arms over his flabby chest. He used to be an athlete in high school and college, but he stopped working out and got fat. His arms are still plenty big, though.

"What's that mean?" he asks. "I know you ain't moving out, especially not without no job."

"Just wait and see."

"Yeah, I'll do that. What did you mean by I should be worried about my own business?"

"Somebody torched your statue."

"Oh, yeah?"

"Yeah, I was over at the bar and somebody burned down your stupid statue."

"Funny no one called me."

"I told them I'd tell you."

"Yeah."

"Wait and see."

"Jesus, I'm gonna be doing a lot of waiting and seeing. What should we do while I'm waiting and seeing?"

"What do you mean?"

"You tell me. You're the one always flirting with me."

"I never flirted with you in my life."

"Yeah, right."

"I hate you. You don't think that's an act, do you?"

He smiles and shakes his head. "You know, you'd almost be pretty if you didn't act like such a bitch all the time."

After he says it, the way he just stares at me makes the light in my room seem too bright. My skin is warm and cold at the same time.

"I'm serious about the statue," I say. "You should call them and see."

He nods like I'm full of shit and looks at my dresser next to the door. He fingers a couple of my rings, and then he picks up one of my hair clips. "You told me to mind my own business. Funny thing is, though, at my business, I hear a lot about your business."

"What are you talking about?"

"Whoever you do your business with, it's their business, too. And if you do your business with enough people and it gets around town, then, hell, it's everybody's business. Hard to have a private life when it involves everybody in the county. And a lot of them people come through my bars. You think I don't hear about shit?"

For a second, I think he's talking about Gary and the preacher, but he's not. He's talking about old shit. "I don't care what you heard," I say. "I never did nothing with you, and I wouldn't do nothing with you. And put my stuff down."

He smells my hair clip. "Oh, you done it with worse then me, ain't you? The story around the bar is that back in school you didn't turn nobody down. You know everybody knows about that night in the back of the BBQ Pit, right? You and, who, every guy that worked there? Boys talk, Sarabeth. They say that by the time the last one got to you, he couldn't even get it up because you was just too goddamn gross to look at."

Outside, a car turns into our lot. Momma? No, she has to work tonight.

The front door opens, and Tommy turns around. "You can't just walk into somebody's house, boy," he says.

"I'm sorry," I hear Gary say down the hall.

"Hey, Gary, I'm back here," I call real loud.

Gary comes up to my bedroom door, but Tommy don't move out of the way.

Gary looks at me. "I just wanted to talk to you," he says.

"Good, I want to talk to you, too."

"He know?" Tommy says, jerking his head at Gary.

"Shut up, Tommy."

"Know what?" Gary says.

He puts down the hair clip. "About your little girlfriend here, Gary. About what all she done."

"Shut up, I said!"

Gary looks back and forth between us. "What's he talking about?" he asks me.

"He's just being an asshole and talking a bunch of shit. Before you walked in here he was trying to get me to blow him or something."

Gary is almost as tall as Tommy, but Tommy's older and meaner. Gary can't really look at him. I think he's afraid.

Tommy smirks. "I never said nothing about no blow jobs, but I heard you give enough of them. Gary, you ever hear about Sarabeth fucking all them guys down at the Pit?"

Gary glances at me, and then he turns and punches Tommy in the face. Tommy staggers back, but once he gets his balance, he jumps on Gary. I scramble over my bed, yelling and running after them as they tumble down the hallway, knocking pictures off the wall. Maybe Gary gets in some hits at first, but after Tommy punches him a couple of times, Gary covers up like a damn kid. Tommy drags him across the living room carpet by his hair and his shirt, and Gary's trying to get to his feet, but Tommy kicks open the screen door and throws him outside.

I swing on Tommy, and he takes the hit and catches my hands. I try to claw his eyes, but he's too strong and holds my wrists. When I try to knee him in the balls, he jerks his leg up and catches it on his thigh.

He shoves me to the floor.

I'm cussing him a wild blue streak when his phone starts blasting a Toby Keith ringtone. Tommy tells me, "Fuck you, you little slut. Why don't you go pick your boyfriend up off the lawn? Best get him out of here before he makes me hurt him for real." Then he answers the phone. "Hey, Frankie, what's up?"

I run outside, and Gary is already standing up, tears coming out of his eyes and blood and snot coming out of his nose.

"I'm sorry," he says, and the shame is all over him for getting his ass kicked in front of me. His voice cracks when he says, "I'll go back in there and kill him if you want me to. I will. I'm not afraid."

My skin turns to ice. Blood is pumping in my ears.

"You really do love me, don't you?" I say. "You really would kill him for me, wouldn't you?"

"Yes."

I shake my head and reach for him, pull him close to me. I tell him, "I love you, too, Gary." And goddamn it, I really do mean it.

FOURTEEN GARY DOANE

I'm still hocking up blood and snot when Tommy runs outside, shoving his phone in his pocket. I try to get in front of Sarabeth because I'm afraid he's going to come at her again, but suddenly, he doesn't care about us at all. He jumps in his truck and tears out of there, his tires spitting gravel.

She asks me if I want to go back inside. But I don't want to be here when Tommy comes back.

Where is there left for us to go? Not my house, not hers. We get in my mom's car, and I let her drive so I can soak up my bloody nose on some napkins in the glove compartment.

We don't say anything for a while. We're both shaking. I don't know what she's over there thinking, but I'm content to let her think it in peace.

I'm not mad anymore. My heart's stopped pounding so bad. My nose feels a little better, too. I touch it with my fingertips. It's stopped bleeding.

Sarabeth says, "You . . . didn't have to do that for me."

I shrug.

"You didn't have to do that for me, but I'm glad you did. I have to get away from here. I hate that motherfucker. God, I hate this whole place."

"Did he touch you? Before I got there?"

"No."

"Has he ever . . ."

"Don't. He never touched me. He was just talking shit."

I tell her, "He's such a piece of fucking garbage. I don't know why your mom is with him."

"Well, she ain't never had taste in men. That's for damn sure."

"Not like you."

"What does that mean?"

"I mean, you're with me."

"Oh." She tries to smile.

"What'd you think I meant?"

"What he was talking about back there. The story about when I worked at the BBQ Pit in high school."

"Oh. No, I meant you got good taste in men 'cause you're with me."

She takes us out to the highway. I don't know where she's going. I bet she doesn't know, either. Sarabeth is the type who just gets in and drives and figures out where she's going later. I admire that about her.

She looks over at me. "You believe what he said back there? That story about me?"

"Let me ask you a question," I say. "Have I ever asked you about it?"

"No."

"You know that story has been around town for years. I mean, you know it has. Have I ever asked you about it?"

"No."

"I ever ask you about *anyone* you've ever been with?"

"No."

"You ever wonder why I never asked?"

"Yes."

"Because I don't care. I do not care. I mean, if you want to tell me, then you should. If you want me to know because it's important to you, then I want to know. Then I do care, because you care. But I don't have any, you know, idle curiosity about it."

She takes a deep breath. "It's true," she says. "About that night after work at the Pit, I mean."

I nod, but I don't say anything.

"There was only three of them," she says, "but everybody thinks it was literally every guy who worked there. I know for a fact that Jimmy Bell told people he was there, but he didn't even work that night. For a while there, though, for like a week or so, it was this big thing to say you was in on the Sarabeth Simmons gangbang. The other boys thought it was all hard-core and shit. But then what happened was, the girls in town didn't like it. No nice Christian girl wants to date a guy who fucked the town slut in a gangbang. So the boys all stopped bragging, and then everybody just kinda forgot about the boys. It's like everybody was in on it and nobody was in on it. Nobody wants to admit they fucked me, so now I'm the slut who never fucked anybody in particular. The boys all got off scot-free, but everybody still looks at me like I'm a piece of shit."

She takes another deep breath and glances over at me.

I say, "I'm sorry."

"For what?"

"For Van Buren County being such a shitty place for you."

She nods. "You heard about it, huh?"

"About that night? Yeah."

"And you really don't care?"

"I care that you got hurt."

She puts her head down. "Gary . . ."

I look back at the road, wanting her to look up at it. Finally, she does look up, and she turns on the signal and pulls off the road. She puts the car in park and leans over and cries in my arms.

"Fuck this place," I say. "You want to know why I went along when you said I should flirt with the preacher? Because fuck this place. He's the king of the hypocrites. He's their big hero and look at what he is. He's nothing but a damn liar."

She looks up at me and nods. "You're right. But what are we going to do?"

"I tell you what we do. We pack up tonight."

"Yes," she says, sitting up. "Hell yes."

"I'm serious."

"Me too. Let's get the fuck out of here. Tonight. But what about the preacher?"

"He's gonna pay us," I say. "He's gonna pay us what he owes us. He's gonna pay us what all these fuckers owe us."

FIFTEEN BRIAN HARTEN

Nineteen thousand, eight hundred and seventy-seven dollars.

I stare at it on my bed, divided up into stacks of hundreds, twenties, tens, fives, and ones. No fifties. Nobody really uses fifties anymore. Sorry, Grant.

Nearly twenty grand sitting on my bed. Most of it is in twenties. Maybe ten thousand bucks just in twenty-dollar bills alone.

I've counted it three times now. After I ditched my clothes and got cleaned up and changed into new clothes, first thing I did was count the cash. Then I counted it again. And again.

Nineteen thousand, eight hundred and seventy-seven dollars.

I walk around all that cash, stare at it, sit down on a chair across from it like I want to have a conversation with it about our future.

I could just keep it. I mean, that's the first thing that comes to mind. The hell with Richard Weatherford and whatever bullshit he's gotten himself into. I made myself nearly twenty grand tonight with five bucks' worth of gas. And now I'm fixing to hand it over to some asshole? And not just *some* asshole. *The* asshole who's keeping me from opening my store and turning my life around. I'm going to commit a crime and then give him the money?

But, okay, then what am I going to do with nearly twenty grand? It's a lot of money, but it ain't a whole lot of money. It won't help me open the store. I guess I could pay off some of my creditors.

But what am I going to do? Pay people back with a stack of twenties? Like that wouldn't be suspicious.

I go over and peek through the blinds. No one.

They'll know it was me.

It could be anyone. But ain't I gonna be the first one they think of? Tommy's not going to know it's me? Of course he is. I'm gonna be the first motherfucker he thinks about.

No, I can't keep this shit. The sooner I get rid of it, the better off I'll be. I'll hand it over to the preacher and that will be that. That way, when the cops come and shake me down, they won't find a thing.

I start packing it up. After I left Tommy's, I ditched the backpack and stuffed the cash in an old Walmart bag from Roxie's floorboard. Now I cram the money back in the bag and wrap it shut with some packing tape. I throw on a jacket even though it's not really cool enough for one, shove the money under my arm, and zip up the jacket. I walk outside with my left arm clamped to my side.

I'm locking my door when Erikson calls me across the parking lot. "Hey, Harten, come here."

He's actually standing in the middle of the parking lot. Can't act like I don't see him. I just give him a wave. "Hey, man, I gotta run."

"Come here."

"Gotta go. No time."

"Get your ass over here," he says. He says it half joking, just dude to dude, but he also seems a little annoyed that I won't come over. "Just take a second."

It'll look weird, me being rude like this. So I go over to him. He's standing behind a couple of my neighbors' cars.

"The hell you wearing a jacket for?" he asks.

"It's a little chilly."

"Not really."

"That why you called me over here, man?"

He shakes his head and points between the cars. There's a cat, gray with stripes, looking back at us.

"What?" I say. "You never saw a cat before?"

"You see his balls?"

"What?"

"Look! I mean, tell me them ain't the biggest pair of cat balls you ever seen."

"I can't see his balls, man."

"Look."

"I am looking, but he's sitting down."

"Here, let me turn him around."

Erikson stomps and claps, and the cat darts away under one of the cars and across the parking lot. Before he disappears behind the apartments, I catch a glimpse of his balls. They're pretty big.

"You see 'em?"

"Yeah, man. They're pretty big."

He smiles like he just proved that God exists.

"When's the last time you even saw a cat with balls?" he says. "I mean, any cat? Everybody's cutting balls off cats morning, noon, and night. But that dude is packing. Mr. Balls, my man."

"Okay, man . . . If we're done gawking at some cat's nutsack, I gotta go."

He nods. "Where you heading?"

"Gotta take Roxie's car back to her."

"Yeah, she came around looking for you."

"What? When?"

"I don't know. Earlier. She going out with Jeff Tramble? They come by in his truck, pulled in, she got out and knocked on your door. When you wasn't here, they left."

"She's looking for her car. I had to borrow it this morning, and I told her I would get it back to her a while ago. She's probably pissed as hell."

"Couldn't get your car outta hock?"

I just shrug that off like I don't want to talk about it, which I don't. "I'll see you later," I say.

"Something wrong with your arm?"

"No."

"Holding it kind of funny."

"I don't know, maybe it's my back. I think I fucked it up this morning when that dude kicked my ass." I glance at my cell like I'm looking at the time. "I gotta go."

He just barely nods and doesn't say anything, but he stares as I walk over to Roxie's car. I get in and fire it up, and I try not to look at him as I'm backing out, but when I get to the edge of the parking lot, just before I turn onto the road and drive away, I check the rearview mirror, and he's still watching me.

———

I drive to the Exxon and use the payphone like a drug dealer in the seventies. The preacher picks up on the second ring.

"Yes?"

"You know who this is?" I ask.

"Mr. Harten."

"Don't say my name, man. Don't you read the papers? NSA and all that shit."

He just mouth breathes into the phone for a while. Then he says, "I don't know what to say, then."

"You want to meet? I got your stuff."

"Where?"

"Same place as last time."

"Okay," he says. "I can meet you tomorrow."

"No, no, no, man. Now. Right fucking now."

"It's after seven. I can't right now."

"Yeah, you can, and you are. Right now. I can't wait. I can't drive around with this shit on me."

"What? Why?"

"Dude, don't ask me questions. You don't want to know the answers anyway. Just meet me. Now."

"I have to have an excuse. I have people who—"

"I have people, too, man. We all have people. You go tell your people whatever the fuck you need to tell them, and then you meet me. You want what I got, you gotta come get it. That's it."

He breathes for a while. Then he says, "Okay. I'll be there as soon as I can."

SIXTEEN RICHARD WEATHERFORD

I slip my phone into my pocket and stare at the carpet. Down the hall, I can hear the children in the kitchen laughing and talking. I don't hear Penny's voice, though I know she is with them. I don't know yet how I should speak to her.

I will have to walk out there and tell them all that I have to run back to the church. It's not such an odd thing to do, for me to work late at the church before a big day like Easter. Penny will know, though. She's already mad at me. I should address the children rather than her.

When I step into the hallway, I run into Johnny.

"Where you going?" I ask.

"Kitchen."

Good. We can walk into together. That will make it look like I've been with him rather than hiding in my office.

Matthew and Mark are at the kitchen table facing each other across some board game. This is their ritual when Matthew's home from school. The games have changed over the years—never video games, which move too quickly for Mark—but always board games, always long, always epic. Risk. Axis and Allies. They once played a game of Monopoly that lasted over a week. I have no idea what they're playing right now.

Penny is leaning against the island while Mary, sitting on the counter, is saying, "Vanessa is a great roommate, but now my whole life is cat hair."

Penny glances in my direction, but she turns back to Mary and tells her, "What's the cat's name again?"

"Jolene."

"After the Dolly Parton song?"

"Yeah," Mary says with a smile. "Anyway, I thought getting off campus would be cool, you know. And Jolene's fun to have around. Really. For a cat, she's pretty sweet. But no matter how much I sweep and dust, there're always these little dirty tumbleweeds of hair blowing across the hardwood floors. Drives me insane. If the Lord wanted to break Pharaoh sooner, he could have just sent a plague of cat hair."

I never let the children have animals. My father always owned two Labrador retrievers, replacing each one as soon as it died, and I grew up in a house filthy with dog hair. As a result, none of my kids have the usual attachment to animals.

"Maybe this plague is a sign," I say with a wry smile.

Mary nods. "First cat hair, then Trump."

"Ugh, I know," Penny says.

"I can't believe he's winning . . ."

Matthew looks up from the game he's playing and tells his sister, "I don't know. I like Cruz, too, but the primary voters are flocking to Trump. If he gets the nomination, I think we need to start reconciling ourselves to voting for him."

Mary says, "He's just so gross."

Matthew nods, but I can tell he wants to argue the point. He can't help himself. Matthew is like me in this way. Neither of us can resist saying something when we know we're in the right. Of the children, he's the most pragmatic, the most political.

He tells her, "Well, unfortunately, the electorate are the ones who get to vote. And if we're going to stop the Dems from putting another activist judge on the Supreme Court, then we're going to have to pull the lever for Trump. For me, it comes down to the realpolitik of the situation. I think he'll gather some good people around him. Plus, I think he makes sense on a lot of stuff, actually. If you really listen to him, not just listen to what people on TV say about him, but listen to *him*, crude as he is, he makes a pretty good case for himself."

Mary shakes her head at this but says nothing.

Johnny looks up at me. "Why do people like Trump, Dad?"

Everyone looks at me to hear what I'll say, even though they already know what I think. We do this as a family; we turn these things over and discuss them. My children's friends have always been amazed to find how close we are as a family, how much we talk and share. We've always discussed things—political, social, personal—as a family. It's not so much that we debate them as much as we examine them and refine our thinking about them. I suppose some outside observer might argue that the children mostly parrot what I say, but Scripture says to train up a child in the way that he should go. I've done just that. And I've done it well.

I say, "It's largely a failure of the Obama administration. There's been a vacuum of leadership at the top so long, and the liberals have stoked so many resentments to stay in power, that it's given room for someone Trump to rise."

The children nod at this, except for Mary. Ever since she went off to college, I've felt her conviction wavering a bit. She hasn't really said anything, but I wonder about her sometimes. I seem to feel her holding back.

Penny folds her arms over her chest and says, "Well, personally, it worries me."

"Why?" Matthew asks her.

"I just don't like him. I think he's using us. A casino owner on his third wife is not my idea of a rock-solid Christian, and I think we need a real Christian in the White House. Now more than ever. That's why I like Cruz."

Matthew says, "Well, sure, I agree, but if comes down to Trump or Hillary?"

Penny shrugs. "Then I'll hold my nose and vote for Trump."

"Really?" Mary asks. "You just said you thought he was using us."

Penny sighs and says, "You don't always get the option of a clean choice, dear."

"I have to go," I say. It comes out a little blunter than I would have liked. I try to be more casual when I follow it up with, "I need to run back up to the church and work on some stuff. I still need to write my sermon for tomorrow."

This announcement barely registers, which is what I want. Everyone nods and goes back to what they were doing. Matthew and Mark return to their game. Penny says something to Mary about Easter dinner. Only Mary smiles at me and says, "Okay, Dad."

For a moment so brief that I barely recognize it, I'm disappointed. *do i want to lie do i want to deceive—* I nod and pat Johnny, who is still at my side, on the head. "Okay, then. I'll be back in a bit."

No one pays me much attention, but Johnny follows me into the darkened living room where I take my coat from the coatrack by the front door.

Standing in the doorway, with the warm light of the kitchen behind him, he asks, "Can I come, Dad?"

"I don't think so, son."

"Please."

"Why do you want to come?"

"I saw a cricket in the baptismal pool the other day. I want to see if it's still there."

I smile. I know, of course, that he just wants to spend some time with me. In a family with five children, face time with the old man is at a premium. "Probably not," I tell him. "I drained the pool myself. No cricket."

"Can I still come with you?"

"It's getting late, son. I don't know how long I'll be up at the church."

Behind him, Penny steps into the doorway. "Johnny, you need to get ready for bed."

He looks back at her. "What time is it?"

She glares at him. "It's time for you to listen to me, that's what time it is."

He lowers his head. "Yes, ma'am."

"Go get ready," she says.

"Yes, ma'am."

As he starts to leave, I say, "I'll double-check on that cricket for you, Johnny."

He makes a show of nodding morosely and leaves us. I notice that instead of heading upstairs to get ready for bed, though, he goes into the kitchen to join his older siblings.

"Gotta go," I tell Penny.

She nods.

I open the front door and walk outside. Beyond the trees, the dying sunlight has dulled to a dusky blue and chilled the air.

Penny follows me to the car, her arms tight to her chest and her shoulders bunched up. In any weather below sweltering, she is always cold, my wife.

"You coming back?" she asks.

I glance around. All our neighbors are indoors, but I feel exposed.

Penny says, "No one's listening to us."

In a low voice, I tell her, "Of course I'm coming back. Stop being ridiculous. You sound utterly ridiculous."

"Do I?"

"Yes. You're the one who was talking about leaving."

"I never said I was leaving."

I sigh and gesture at the open air between our home and the homes of all our neighbors. "This really the best time and place to discuss it?"

She twists her mouth, chewing at the inside of her cheek. It's a nervous habit she's had since childhood, though it has come and gone over the years. "I'll go with you," she says.

"What?"

"Wait for me to get my coat, and I'll go with you to the church."

"Why do you want to come with me to the church?"

"I thought this wasn't the best time and place to discuss it. So, let's go up to the church, which is empty, and let's sit down and discuss it."

My mouth is dry when I say, "Let's talk about it tomorrow."

She stares at me. She stops chewing her cheek. "That's what I thought," she says, and turns and walks back into the house.

As I drive to the car wash, I pass two people I know. One is a man named Fred Stiverson. He attended our church for a while. Fred's been married eight times, and wife number six was a member of our church. After they broke up—when Fred left her for the woman who would become wife number seven—he stopped coming to church. The other person I see is a teenager named Darcy Pruitt. She's a senior this year and plays on the basketball team. Mary played on the same team before she graduated, and she and Darcy were friendly. Darcy's family are Methodists.

Fred is driving his current wife's car, which looks new. Darcy is driving her father's truck, an old junker spitting black clouds of exhaust.

Two people. Two people in the five minutes it takes me to get from my house to the car wash. Two people who know me.

It makes me wonder if anyone else knows about my relationship with Gary. People see things. People talk. If Gary told one person, that would be enough. I'm protected by the fact that he doesn't really have friends left in town. But still, people see things. What if someone else knows? I could never pay off everyone who might know. But I can't think about such things now, can't think about who might know and who might find out. I have to get Gary away from here; then everything will be fine.

And as for Penny . . .

I don't know. *did i waste your life did i make you waste your life on a man who could never love you*— I will deal with her tomorrow. I will recommit to her. I can be the husband she wants, the husband she deserves. I have been that man before. I can be him again. Just as soon as I do this.

<hr>

Harten is waiting for me under the single lamp at the car wash on the hill. I pull up and leave my lights on when I get out of the car. He's dressed differently from this morning, but he looks somehow more disheveled, as if he took off dirty clothes and put on even dirtier ones.

He holds out a messy block of tape and plastic and, I assume, money.

"I got it," he says.

My heart pounds in my ears, and there is a pain starting just behind my right eye. "Good," I say. I lift my hand to take the money, but he pulls it back.

"Couple of things, first," he says. "One thing is, I could only get nineteen thousand."

It's as if there is a swelling behind my eye. I rub it, but doing so makes the pain worse.

"I need thirty."

"Well, you got nineteen."

"That's not what we discussed."

He shrugs. "Tough shit, man. I have nineteen grand in my hand. You can have it, or you can leave with nothing. I can't pull another eleven thousand bucks out of my ass."

I nod. I can make nineteen thousand dollars work. I can issue Gary essentially the same ultimatum that Brian Harten has issued me.

"Okay," I say.

"Good. Second thing is I got this money through illegal means."

"Brian, I don't want to—"

"Yeah, but I want you to know, man. I stole this money from Tommy Weller. Okay? And the cops are gonna come talk to me about it. I can guaran-fucking-tee you that. And when they do, I'm gonna say that I don't know a fucking thing about it. And I'm gonna say I was with you."

"Wait, Brian—"

"No, that's the deal, man. You put me up to this, so you're gonna be my alibi. Me and you were at your church discussing the dry vote."

"Don't you think drawing attention to the two of us is a bad idea?"

"No, I don't think it's a bad idea. If I thought it was a bad idea, I wouldn't have fucking suggested it, would I? It's like you said: you're respectable, and I'm a low-class piece of shit. Well, I'm gonna borrow some of your respectableness."

"If the police already suspect it was you who stole the money, Brian, and then you tell them that we were together, it will make the final part, the part *you* want—the part where I swing the drinking vote your way—it will make that part almost impossible."

Brian nods, but not as if he's agreeing with me; he nods as if he was right about something. "Yeah, well," he says, "here's the thing: at some point either tonight or tomorrow, the cops are gonna come to my door and ask me where I was when Tommy's money got swiped. And I'm gonna tell them I was with you. Now, when they go to you and ask you if you was with me, if you say, 'No,' they're gonna come *back* to me. And at that point, my friend, I am gonna start telling the truth, the whole truth, and nothing but the truth."

"I see."

"Yeah, you see."

"Will they believe it?"

"Don't know. And I don't really care. I'm just gonna tell the truth and see what happens. At that point, I won't have shit to lose by telling the truth."

What can I say? I know he's right. I nod my consent.

"That's what I thought," he says. He holds out the money. "You and me were together tonight from six to seven. Hung out for a while talking about the vote."

I rub my face. My skin is wet with perspiration, yet my flesh is cold to the touch.

"Okay," I say, reaching for the money.

SEVENTEEN PENNY WEATHERFORD

My mother was not a beautiful woman. Clothes, hair, and makeup couldn't change that fact, either. She wasn't ugly, just unremarkable, and I think that's what hurt her the most. The destiny of mediocrity. To make matters worse, she seemed to regard beauty as if it were a moral accomplishment. That made her a harsh judge of unattractive women, and it made her wholly unforgiving of beautiful women who lost their beauty. I remember seeing Elizabeth Taylor on television when the faded star was older and overweight, and my mother saying, "Ugh, turn the channel. She used to be the most beautiful woman in the world, and now look at her." My mother believed in surfaces. She taught me how to keep a home and stay in shape. She taught me that a wife and mother should always look like a wife and mother. She taught me that surfaces matter.

She never liked Richard. They never fought, of course. They stayed polite. But she regarded him as insubstantial, one of the few people who ever regarded him as such. Mother was raised Primitive Baptist, and though she became a Southern Baptist when she married my father, deep down she held on to some of those old hard-shell beliefs. Primitive Baptists believe in the doctrine of irresistible grace, the belief that God predetermines whom he will save, and they believe that you know the saved by the clear righteousness of their actions. Primitive Baptists believe in surfaces, too, I guess.

So why didn't she like Richard? He's better at presenting himself to people than almost anyone I've ever met. She should have loved him. He was attractive, smart, and he held all the correct religious, political, and personal views. Yet she stayed cool toward him until the day she died.

I always told myself she was just jealous, that she resented Richard for taking away her only daughter. For his part, Richard simply wrote it off as the old mother-in-law cliché, and once we were married and Matthew was born, he stopped caring what she thought about him one way or another. In his mind, I became his wife rather than her daughter. And, in fairness, I thought of it the same way. I thought of being a wife the way she taught me to think of being a wife. I sided with my husband, and I chalked up her dislike of him to jealousy and snobbery. No son-in-law would have been good enough for her, I told myself.

But now I wonder.

What would you say if you were here? What did you see in him that worried you?

~

I go upstairs to my room. Before I've even reached my bed, Mary knocks on my door. "Mom?"

"Yes?"

"Can I come in?"

I check my face in the mirror above my dresser. "Yes."

She opens the door and closes it behind her.

"Is everything okay?"

"What do you mean?"

"You seem upset."

"Do I?"

"Yes. You and Dad have both seemed upset today. Is everything okay?"

"I'm not upset," I tell her.

Mary nods, leaning against the door. She's a smart girl. And she's got a good heart. I'm proud of her for being sensitive enough to intuit that her father and I are in a bad way. The rest of my brood downstairs is, I'm sure, oblivious.

But it's none of her business.

"It's nothing you need to worry about, sweetie."

"So there *is* something wrong."

"Don't take that tone with me, Mary."

"What tone?"

"The 'ah ah, I caught you' tone, like you just tripped me up. If I'm having an issue with your father, then I'll take it up with him when he gets home. It doesn't concern you."

She frowns. "Okay, excuse me for asking. I was just trying to help."

"If I *ever* need your help with my marriage, Mary, I'll let you know."

Her face flushes as pink as if I'd slapped her. "Okay," she says, almost starting to cry. "I'm sorry. I was just worried when Dad had that attack this morning."

I take a breath. I nod. Of course. I hadn't thought about what this day must have looked like through her eyes. "Is that what you're worried about?"

"Well, yes, partly."

"He's fine, dear. He'll see the doctor on Monday just to be sure, but I really think he's okay."

"Okay."

I walk over and give her a hug. She doesn't hug me back. "Hey, I'm sorry I snapped at you. I didn't realize that's what you were talking about."

"Everything else is okay?"

"What do you mean?"

"I don't know. I just noticed you stayed in your room a lot today."

"Have I?"

"Seems like it."

"I'm fine. Just a little tired. Okay?"

"Okay," she says. She's still stunned by my earlier curtness, and I realize I must have given her the look my children long ago dubbed "The

Harbinger of Doom." She turns to leave. "Daddy's working late tonight?" she asks.

"Yes," I say, as naturally as if I still thought it was the truth.

Have I been hiding in my room today? Maybe. It's true I don't want to see any of the children right now. Since my fight with Richard this afternoon, I feel like we're both lying to the kids. Every word out of my mouth feels like a lie.

Mary saw through me. But what did she see? Problems between her father and me? That could mean anything. Despite the fact we've tried to keep our fights out of the living room and the kitchen, the kids are not strangers to tension between us. This is not the first time I've taken to my room while Richard took to his car.

Where does he go?

No, don't ask yourself that. There's nothing for you there. He drives around, or he goes up to the church. He runs to the Walmart or he goes to Pickett's.

This town's too small for him to do anything else.

Isn't it?

We've had sex twice since Ruth was born. Do you really think he's not having sex? This town's not too small to keep secrets. Five minutes in any direction is nothing but trees and dirt roads.

Besides, you know he hasn't lost his libido entirely. You know he lied about that.

A few months ago, I came home early from choir practice, and I heard him in our bathroom. Moans, low but unmistakable, and the soft slap of his flesh. At first, I was embarrassed, as if I'd invaded his privacy, knowing that he would have been humiliated to know that I discovered him doing something that he thought he was doing in secret.

Then I was angry and ashamed. Angry because when he stopped touching me, he told me he'd lost his libido entirely. Ashamed, because it had been years since I'd questioned that lie. I suppose I wanted it to be true. It was easier to think he'd lost all interest in sex than to think he'd simply lost interest in me.

Later that night, I looked on his phone and his computer for pornography. Nothing. Either he doesn't look at it or he's better at hiding it than I am at finding it.

Or maybe he doesn't need it. Maybe there's someone else.

Is he having an affair? Have I been a complete fool? Why would he do something so stupid and reckless?

I can feel my face get hot. He hasn't touched me in years. To know that he might be with someone this minute fills me with a rage that makes me dizzy.

Someone knocks on the door.

"What?" I say. "Come in."

Mary again. She pokes her head in. "Ruth says she's been texting you. She's ready to come home."

"Could you go pick her up?"

"At Scarlett's house?"

"Yes."

"Okay."

She closes the door.

I yell, "Mary!"

She opens the door. "Yeah?"

Swinging my legs off the bed, I tell her, "Never mind, I'm going to go get her myself."

Before I go to Scarlett's house to pick up Ruth, I drive down the hill, heading in the opposite direction. I drive over the bridge and go by the church.

Brother Weatherford's car is not there. That's how I think of it. *Brother Weatherford's car is not at the church.* I turn off the service road and swing back toward the church. I want to make sure he's not parked around back or under the trees where I might not see his car. I want to give him the benefit of that doubt. Maybe I'm just imagining things.

But no.

He's not at the church.

"Where are you, Brother Weatherford?" I ask.

After I pick up Ruth at Scarlett's house, she's chattering incessantly. She and Johnny are my youngest children, and they're different from the older three. The older three are almost a separate family. They grew up together, with Matthew and Mary taking care of Mark. They're closer to one another. Johnny and Ruth aren't just younger than the other three, they're both more desperate for attention. On a daily basis, Ruth wants to tell me every single detail of everything that happens to her.

She's giving me a verbatim recitation of the conversations she had with her friend this afternoon. I'm pretending to listen when something slips through.

Ruth says, "Scarlett asked me if you're a preacher."

"What?"

"She asked me if you're a preacher like Daddy."

"What'd you say?"

"I said no."

I don't respond, but something about that pisses me off.

Ruth asks, "You're not a preacher, right?"

"No, but as your father's wife I have a certain position in the church. Haven't you noticed that?"

"What do you mean?"

"People respect me. I teach a Sunday school class. I lead VBS. I'm the chair of the Ladies' Auxiliary. You know that, right?"

Ruth stares out the window. "Yeah," she says. She considers all that. Then she says, "I said you help Daddy run the church."

"Is that what you said?"

"Yes."

"That's right. I help your father run the church. The same way we both run the family."

"But Daddy's in charge, right?"

I glance at my daughter, her smooth little brow furrowed as she tries to put all these pieces together to create a picture of the world she can understand.

I take a deep breath.

"Yes," I say.

My mother only respected a surface she couldn't see through. The whole point of presenting a face to the world, after all, is to convince the world that it's your real face.

The hardest part of adjusting to married life, for me, was reconciling the public and the private in the man I married. Not that Richard was radically different at home than he was at church. He didn't drink or beat me or scream at the kids. From the start, he was a good husband and father. He was a family man. He brought home a paycheck. He lived a clean life.

And yet how can I reconcile the man everyone loves and respects with the man who makes me feel this way? When we walk into church tomorrow morning for Easter Sunday, Richard and I will be two of the most prominent citizens in this town. I'll be hugged and kissed and prayed for tomorrow morning. I know the dress, purple and white, that I'll wear. And I take comfort in this knowledge. It's sure ground beneath my feet. It's my life, the only life I know, the only life I want.

But I haven't loved Richard in years. I can do many things for this marriage. I can put on a good face for the world, and I can bear babies and raise children. I can choke down my pride and humble myself if that's what it takes to maintain the face of Sister Penny Weatherford. Like my mother taught me, the whole point of presenting a face to the world is to convince the world that it's real, because in doing so, it becomes your real face. But the one thing I can't do—the one thing I won't do—is love him. I'll stay with him, but my pride won't let me love a man who doesn't love me back.

EIGHTEEN BRIAN HARTEN

I drop off Roxie's car and split before she can run outside and chew my ass out. That's the smart move. I don't want to have to talk to her, and I don't want to spend any more time in her car with the cops out looking for me. But I'm fucking beat now, and all I want to do is have a drink and go to bed.

Still, when I get to my place, I come up through the woods to look things over before I go waltzing back into my apartment. Everything is nice and quiet. No cops. Neighbors ain't gawking out their windows. Jack shit is going on.

As much as I just want to go down there, though, I hold back and check things out. I'm jittery, like I've been shotgunning coffee all day. I give my hands a shake, stomp my feet.

Sun's gone down, and everything looks cold in the moonlight. A few cars in the lot. A few lights on in apartment windows. But mostly it's just quiet. Erikson's not outside perving on some cat's ballbag, so that's a plus.

I take a breath and walk out of the woods, pine needles crunching under my feet. Across the parking lot, I rush as quietly as I can up to my door. I should have left the light on when I left. Unlock the door and slip inside. Hit the light. Lock the door behind me and wait.

"Hello?" I say.

Nothing.

I walk into the kitchen to grab a beer. I'm out.

I go to the bedroom and hit the light and my guts explode.

I drop. Lunch spikes up to my mouth.

"Cocksucker," he says. "Fucking cocksucker." Hits me in the back. Hard. Wood. A bat.

I cover up, trying not to get hit in the head. But he doesn't go for the head. He doesn't want to fuck me up. Not yet. He hits me in the thighs.

"Tommy—"

"Shut up and stay down."

"Tommy, look, I—"

"You got shit in your ears, you fucking cocksucker? You shut your fucking mouth."

I shut up.

"Lean against the bed."

I push myself against the bed and try to look up at him, but the bulb on the ceiling fan is like a goddamn interrogation light. He dives at me like he's going to bite my face. "Where's my money?"

I shake my head, but before I can even think of a lie he pulls back and whacks me in the shin. I scream, and my lunch pumps up to my mouth again. Gag, one hand over my mouth, the other on my leg.

"This ain't the CIA," Tommy says. "I ain't got all night to waterboard you. I'm just gonna beat your ass until you give me my money. And if that don't work . . ." He pats his side, and I see that he's wearing his Glock clipped to his belt.

"Gonna vomit," I manage to choke out.

"You puke on me, I swear to Christ I'll knock your teeth out." He's breathing hard, his big gut heaving and sticking out the bottom of his pink polo. Got the bat in one hand, with the other hand on his doughy hip.

I double over, holding my leg. My shin might be broke.

He watches. Shakes his head. "I can't believe you did this. Are you fucking stupid, Harten? I never took you for stupid. Not this stupid. You really thought you was gonna steal from me and that was gonna be it? No consequences?"

"Are the cops coming?" I manage to ask.

"Yeah. They're right behind me. Told me to go ahead and break into your house with a baseball bat and a gun."

I hold my shin like it's about to fall apart.

"Where's my money?" he says. "And don't tell me you spent it to get your car back, 'cause I just saw you walk out of the woods like a fucking hillbilly."

"I don't have it."

He lifts the bat.

"Please," I say, and tears come to my eyes.

"Are you crying?" he says. He raises both his eyebrows. "I wanna laugh at you, Harten, but, Christ Almighty, I think I'm more fucking offended than anything else."

I hate it. I hate the tears. Ever since I was a kid, I couldn't help the tears. They just come up in moments when I'm scared or really upset. I'm not a pussy. I just can't stop the tears.

"I'm not crying."

"Looks like crying from where I'm standing."

"I tear up. It ain't the same thing."

"Tell it to your gynecologist. Only thing I want to hear from you is where you got my money hid."

"I had to give it to someone."

"Who?"

I don't know why I hold back the preacher's name. I don't owe him anything. Certainly don't got a reason to take a beating for him. He's the reason I'm in trouble. He's the reason for all my troubles.

I hesitate for a second, though. Maybe I'm just scared. I don't know what will happen once I say his name.

But Tommy's lifting the bat . . .

"Weatherford! Richard Weatherford!"

He makes a face like I farted. "What? Bullshit."

"I swear to fucking God, man."

"The preacher?"

"Yes."

"You sure you didn't mail it to Billy Graham?"

"I swear to God. Why would I make that up? Why would I say I gave it to him if it wasn't the truth?"

"The hell does that mean?"

"I mean, if I was gonna lie, I wouldn't say the money was for Richard Weatherford. I'd say it was for loan sharks or something like that."

"He told you to rob me?"

"No. I just had to come up with some money for him."

"Why?"

I grab the edge of the bed to pull myself up. My stomach feels like a fishbowl. "I just need one second, man. One second. You fucking hammered me in the guts. I probably got internal bleeding."

Tommy doesn't say anything, but he lowers the bat. "You gave the money to Richard Weatherford," he says, turning it over in his head. "So you stole money from me to, what? Bribe him? This about the vote?"

"It wasn't my idea. He called me today. Said he wanted to meet to discuss the vote. I figured what the hell, so I go meet him. That's when he tells me that he needs some cash, off the books. I don't know why, and he won't say why. But he needs cash."

Tommy leans against the wall. "And he told you that if you get him the money he needs . . ."

"Then he'll swing the vote my way."

"You believed that?"

"Yeah . . ."

"That's what you get for listening to a preacher. They're worse than politicians. No honest man talks for a living."

"I know, but—"

"The preacher of the biggest Baptist church in the county told you he was going to swing the dry vote into a wet vote, and you really thought he could do that?"

"Sure, why not?"

"Because if he'd tried it, they'd crucify him, that's why. What's he gonna do next, marry a couple of fags? A preacher like Weatherford ain't some cult leader. He can't just make shit up out of thin air. He's gotta tell his people the same shit their momma's been telling them their whole life. And you know what the Baptists been telling their kids for a hundred fucking years? That alcohol comes straight out of Satan's asshole."

I shrug. "I was desperate, man."

"Why does he need the money?"

"Hell if I know."

"Maybe he got somebody pregnant and he's got to shut her up. Or gambling? No, not gambling. But maybe he lost his ass on some business deal . . ."

I just shrug again.

Tommy's tapping the bat against his leg. "When did you give him the money?"

"Just now."

"Where?"

"Up at the little car wash over on Huddo."

"There was about twenty grand?"

"Nineteen and some change."

He just stares at me.

"What?" I ask.

"Shut up," he says.

He's thinking. That's fine. I just hold myself. Can't decide which hurts worse, my guts or my shin. They both feel busted.

"Call him," Tommy says.

I start to tell him that the preacher told me never to call, but I think better of it and dig my phone out of my pocket. I nearly cut my hand on the broken screen. It's glowing, but the display is just a bunch of fucked-up white lines.

"Goddamn it, you broke my cell, man."

He just stares at me.

I stare at the smashed phone. It's my whole business. All the numbers and info I need. Ray had the laptop. I've been running my life out of this thing, and now it's all busted to shit.

My life is busted to shit.

Tommy shrugs. "Tough. You shouldn't have set fire to my property. You shouldn't have stole from me like a bitch. Get up."

"What? Why?"

"Just get up."

"Dude, you don't have to hit me again, okay? I get that I'm screwed. I'm cooperating. Hitting me some more is just going to make me useless to you."

He nods. "I know. So get up."

Using the bed, I pull myself up. I get to my feet with my guts churning and my leg feeling like it's splintering.

"Let's go," he says.

"Where we going?"

"Where do you think?" he says. "We're gonna go get my money."

NINETEEN RICHARD WEATHERFORD

The Walmart parking lot is half full, and I've already seen one family from our church pull up and go inside while I've been sitting in my minivan staring at my phone. Staring at my phone and waiting.

Gary won't answer my calls. I don't want to leave a message or a text, so I don't know what to do.

What I want is to go home and go to bed, because I'm suddenly so exhausted I can barely sit up straight in the seat.

But my glove compartment is full of the evidence of a crime. It's not much money, but it doesn't have to be a lot. It's enough, those few thousand dollars, that envelope full of paper, to ruin my career, my marriage, my life.

I call Gary again. Nothing. Just a generic voicemail beep.

I don't leave a message. What else can I do but keep calling or go home and try to find him tomorrow?

No, not tomorrow. This day has been enough of a disaster. Besides, on Easter Sunday it would be impossible for me to disappear for even a few minutes. That means I would have to keep this money for least another forty-eight hours, and that's unacceptable. This has to end tonight.

Which means that there is only one thing left to do.

I put the car in drive and head over to Gary's house.

Along either side of the empty highway, the illuminated windows of simple homes shine out from the trees. I know the names of almost all the people who live in these houses, and I know many—maybe even most—of these people personally. They all know my name, my reputation.

i knew thee in thy mother's womb

I shake my head, unable to think about the larger ramifications of what I'm doing. I simply don't have the time for that right now. I'm drowning, and drowning men don't call out for God. They gasp for air.

Gary's parents will probably be home. Jill and Vaughn Doane. A quiet couple. They're members of the church, though they're sporadic in their attendance. I expect them to make an appearance tomorrow for Easter.

But what kind of people are they? What should I prepare for?

Vaughn has always seemed like an affable man. He works over at the Bill Linn Chevrolet as a salesman, and I assume he's good at that job. I know that Jill teaches high school English, but I forget where. I think she's got a bit of a commute to somewhere north of here, a smaller town with a smaller school. I've always gotten the sense that she's not terribly happy attempting to teach the classics of English literature to roomfuls of defiantly ignorant rednecks.

It was Vaughn who asked me to talk to Gary after he dropped out of school. I got the sense that reaching out to me was the last thing the Doanes thought to try, which tells me a lot about how they see me.

I assume they like me, but I don't know how much interest either of them has in church. I remember that they attended my eight-week Bible study series "God's Plan for Financial Victory." Because America's contribution to Christian thought is the idea that a God that won't promise to make you rich isn't a God worth serving, the reality is that a portion of my congregation can only think of life—even the Christian life—in material terms. The Doanes seem like this type of Christian.

What that tells me is that I have to approach them casually. These are the kind of people who want a preacher to be conventional, useful, and, above all, undemanding. I'm here to serve them, never to ask anything of them.

They live in a cul-de-sac alongside five or six other homes. I once drove past their house to see if Gary was there. It was a stupid, reckless thing to do. People had to have seen my car and wondered why the preacher was on their street. To cover my tracks, I stopped at another house to visit an elderly shut-in, a lady who had not been to our church in many years. She was ecstatic to see me.

This time, however, I cannot be subtle. I turn onto the road and drive right up to the Doane house. Vaughn's car is in the driveway.

I grab the copy of the Bible that I keep in the car and get out and don't waste time getting to the door. I ring the doorbell.

I rarely drop in on people unannounced. Dropping in on people unannounced is, after all, something of a throwback to the days before cell phones and social media. There's a palpable sense of confusion from inside the house. *Was that the doorbell? Yes. Who could that be?* Luckily, while an unannounced visitation from the preacher is rarely welcomed, it is not unheard of. The Doanes have probably been dreading such a visit for years.

Finally, the door opens, and Vaughn greets me with a smile. "Brother Richard," he exclaims, as if he's excited to see me. "Well, how are you, sir?"

We shake hands. His handshake is vigorous. I say, "Vaughn, I'm excellent. Hope I'm not disturbing your Saturday night."

"Oh, no. We were just watching a little Netflix." He steps back. "C'mon in."

He leads me down a long clean hallway. The end of the hallway opens into a large sunken den where Jill is sitting on the sofa in front of a flat-screen television. On the screen, a well-dressed man and woman are sharing drinks in what looks like a hotel bar.

"Honey," Vaughn says, "turn that off. We've got company."

The hurry to shut off the television upon my entrance into a home is something that never fails to amuse me. It seems as if everyone I visit is in the middle of watching something they don't want me to see.

"Brother Richard," Jill says, turning off the television as she gets to her feet. She leaves it at that, at my name. She doesn't take a step toward me and does not extend a hand.

"Jill, how are you?"

She nods. Then after a moment, she says, "I'm fine." She looks at her husband.

Vaughn smiles at me. "Can I get you a glass of water? Or a Coke?"

"Oh, no, thank you. I'm fine. Just wanted to drop in and say howdy. Haven't checked in on you all in a little while, and I was around, so I thought I'd see how you're doing."

"We're good," Vaughn says. "Good. Things at the dealership have been doing pretty well."

"Selling a lot of cars?"

"Trying to," he says with a laugh.

I laugh, too.

Jill Doane smiles. Barely.

"How about you, Jill?"

She raises her eyebrows. "Still fighting the good fight."

"Not easy teaching grammar in the Ozarks, I bet."

She genuinely smiles at that. "*Teaching Grammar in the Ozarks* sounds like the title of a memoir."

Vaughn nods. "You should write that book."

"That could get you on the Oprah book club," I say.

"It would be a harrowing tale," she says.

As we're all politely laughing at that, I look around very naturally and ask, "Is Gary around? I'd like to say hi to him, too."

"No, I'm sorry," Vaughn says. "You missed him."

"Oh, that's okay. How's he doing these days?"

Vaughn gestures me to the sofa, and we sit down. Jill takes the love seat, her hands in her lap.

"He's been doing okay," Vaughn tells me. "But we still worry about him, of course."

Vaughn begins to tell me the reasons for their most recent concerns about Gary. Of course, most people in town know about Gary's problems. Vaughn came up to my office not long after his son was kicked out of school, and we prayed for Gary. The following week the Doane family began regularly attending services for the first time. They only lasted a couple of months, but it was in that time that I began to notice Gary in a way I never had before. I would find him looking at me, and not the way that most of my congregants do. He seemed to be studying me, as if he couldn't care less about the eternal truths I was imparting because he was too distracted by *me*. He seemed always to be looking past the face I presented to the world, effortlessly seeing something in me that was obscured even to my wife and children.

As Vaughn Doane is telling me about his hopes for his son's future, as Jill Doane listens intently, as I nod and respond with concern and compassion—I catch my reflection in the full-length mirror at the end of the hallway. It's pure Crate & Barrel, but I remember Gary telling me about it, about how much his mother loves it.

I can see my mouth move. I can see the compassion in my eyes as I offer to pray with them. For the first time, I can see the mask that Gary can see through so easily. I can't see through it, though. What does Gary see that I don't?

When I pray with the Doanes for their son, I close my eyes and I hear the words *Dearest Heavenly Father, we come to you now to ask*, but I am divided between the me that is speaking and the me that is listening. I have prayed thousands of prayers, but I have never felt further from God.

When I finish *In Jesus's name, Amen*, we open our eyes, and I say, "Well, I should get going. I hope to see you folks at service tomorrow. The choir has a beautiful set of songs worked up. I know you'll find it a blessing."

Vaughn says, "We'll be there. We'll be sure to bring Gary, too. Even if I have to drag him."

As an afterthought or a small bitter joke, Jill says, "Maybe if we ask that girlfriend of his to come with us, he'll follow her."

"What?"

"His girlfriend." She searches my face. "Has he not mentioned her to you?"

"You know, I'm not sure . . . What was her name, again?"

"Sarabeth Simmons."

"I don't believe I know her."

Jill says, "Her mama is Carmen Fuller. I'm not sure where the 'Simmons' comes from. I guess Carmen was married at some point."

"She was married to some guy over in Cave City," Vaughn says. "That was just after high school."

"Anyway," Jill says, her voice becoming conspiratorial, as if she's about to share a nasty secret, "Carmen's living with Tommy Weller now."

"And this Sarabeth and Gary are seeing each other?"

"I suppose," Vaughn says. "But Gary won't say much about it. He made us promise not to tell our friends about it. Says he doesn't want people to gossip about him. Says there's enough gossip about him after he dropped out of school the way he did." He scratches his head. "Of course, since you can't keep a secret in this town, I assumed everyone already knew."

"I didn't know," I say.

"Right. I guess that's true."

"Maybe Gary's not the topic of gossip he thinks he is," Jill says.

"I suppose not," I say.

I reach out and shake hands with Vaughn. I almost lean in to hug Jill, but she extends her hand, so I shake with her instead. I tell them I'll see them tomorrow.

As I pass the big mirror, my reflection flickers by, trying to catch my eye. I say so long to Vaughn as he closes the door behind me. I walk out to my car, get in, and back out of their driveway.

I drive to the end of the road and stop at the intersection.

And I sit there.

Gary has a girlfriend?

I don't . . .

I drive. I don't really know where. I drive on instinct, on rote memory. Houses, businesses, signs—all fragments of my daily life that seem disconnected—pass by as quickly as my reflection in the hallway mirror. I know I know them all, but none of them seem to hold any meaning.

Why would he have a girlfriend? He's gay.

Why would he not tell me he has a girlfriend?

Elliptical moonlight through clusters of pines. A two-story house with a limp American flag in the yard and a car up on blocks in the driveway. A truck blasts me with high beams because my brights are on.

There's no reason for Gary to conceal a girlfriend from me. And concealing her is what he must be doing. I would know if he had a girlfriend. Nothing happens in the daylight here that is not known to one and all.

But that cliché about how everyone knows everyone else's business in a small town is simply not true. Secrets grow in the dark, and there is plenty of darkness in these trees.

So why is Gary hiding a girlfriend from me?

He's afraid I would be jealous?

You fool, he would have to care about you to be afraid of your jealousy.

I swing off the road and skid to a stop in the mud and grass.

I stare my knuckles, white and freckled, gripping the steering wheel. Another truck passes me, and as its lights fill my car, I catch my reflection in the rearview mirror. Turning on the overhead light, I flip down the vanity mirror to look at my face, trying to see what Gary must see. I don't see a preacher, a child of God, a husband, a father. I just see skin and hair against meat and bone. My face is lined and the flesh is both too soft and too rough. Bumps and moles have started to appear, along with strange discolorations. I am a middle-aged man. Soon enough, I will be an old man. And then I will be dead. And none of it matters. Why should it? How could it?

That boy never cared a thing for me. That is clear to me now, as clear as this aging face of mine. When Gary looks at me, he sees nothing but age and foolishness, a foolishness compounded by age. I see it now, too, but he saw it first. He always saw it.

So why did he hide a girlfriend from me?

Because they're up to something. Jill Doane doesn't like the girl, and Jill seems to be a wary judge of character.

Gary has a secret girlfriend, and this morning he called me up and demanded that I give him money to leave town.

Look at yourself, you old fool. You were sloppy, shortsighted, stupid. He played on that. They *played on that.* Gary and this girl have conspired to blackmail me. It's as simple and as tawdry as that. They set me up, like Potiphar's wife.

He never wanted me.

Did they laugh about it? Are they waiting for the money right now, laughing about it?

I pick up the phone and call him.

Before the voicemail beeps, I take a calm breath.

"Hi, Gary. This is Brother Weatherford from First Baptist Church. I just had a nice visit with your parents, and I thought I would reach out to see if you would like to perhaps meet up sometime and visit. I'd love to have the opportunity to talk with you and pray with you. Call me back, okay? God bless you, son."

As I wait, I have to shake my head. How could I have chosen to ignore what was right in front of me all the time? When we first started talking, Gary complained about his parents, but I suspect all of that was a lie, or, at best, an exaggeration. Jill might be a bit chilly, but she loves her son as much as Vaughn does. Gary played me—he and his girlfriend.

Sarabeth Simmons.

I do recall her now, vaguely. She was one of the ill-parented pieces of white trash that occasionally blows into church and lands in the youth group until the next gust of wind sweeps them away. I remember nothing of any importance about her except some tawdry whispers of a late-night orgy. People don't share the details of those kinds of rumors with me, but I know it was her. The girl who works the checkout at Pickett's. And all this time the little whore's been laughing at me.

I glance at my phone. Gary hasn't called me back, which is good because I know I'm not ready to confront him—them—yet. I don't know what to do. I need to clear my mind. Maybe I'll go back up to the church, just to have somewhere to sit and think. I wish I had more time. Hours, days, even. I haven't had time to think about this, and Gary and Sarabeth have had . . . well, I don't know, do I? They could have been planning this for a long time.

She's the daughter of Carmen Fuller. I know nothing about Carmen except that she cuts hair part-time at a salon in town.

And she lives with Tommy Weller . . .

Which means there's a connection between Sarabeth and Tommy Weller. Tommy Weller, who Brian Harten robbed today.

I catch my reflection again in the vanity mirror. As I look at myself this time, however, I think of my picture on our church website. Brother Richard Weatherford, wearing a suit, smiling and confident, a man of God ready to help. That's what people see. It's all that anyone in this town can see when they look at my face, this mask that's been years in the making. I've married these people and baptized their children and chastised their wayward teenagers and buried their aged parents. That's what they see. When they look at me, they just see the preacher, a man with no obvious connection to any of this tawdry unpleasantness.

And what do they see when they look at the other people at the center of this mess? A tavern owner. His disgruntled ex-employee. A depressed college dropout. And the town slut.

TWENTY SARABETH SIMMONS

I turn onto Gary's street.

"Think they're still awake?"

"Maybe," he says. "But maybe not. They're both early-to-bed people, and they're going to church tomorrow. So maybe we'll get lucky."

"If they see you all busted up, they're gonna shit."

"I know. I'll go in quiet. I know how to get in without waking them up. My dad could sleep through an earthquake, and my mom won't get up even if she hears me."

I pull up to his house and keep the car going. He gets out and doesn't close his door all the way. Then he walks up to the house, unlocks the front door, and goes inside.

It's quiet on Gary's street. I like it. Tommy's place is too far out in the boonies. I want to live in a city. I'd rather hear cars and sirens and people fighting than to have to listen to the bugs chirping and the branches creaking in the night. You never know what's out in the woods.

I look at the other houses. A couple of lights are on in the windows. One house has a yard light shining on a MAKE AMERICA GREAT AGAIN sign that I guess stays lit up 24/7. The house next to it doesn't have a yard light, but I can kind of make out a Hillary sign in the dark. I wonder if the people in them houses like each other.

The front door of Gary's house opens, and he walks out. He's hurrying, but he's not running or anything. Once he gets in, I back up and get us out of there, but I don't peel out or anything. Nice and easy.

"How'd it go?"

"I think my mom was awake. I saw the light under her door."

"She say anything?"

"No."

"She didn't get up to check on you?"

"She's not exactly the 'get up to check on you' type."

"Oh. Okay."

He's got a backpack full of stuff.

I ask him, "You bring clothes to sleep in?"

"Yes."

"Bring your toothbrush?"

He smiles at me. He's still got dried blood and dirt on him, but he smiles like a damn kid. "You're sweet, Sarabeth."

I get on the highway going back to Tommy's, so I can pack my stuff and Gary can get cleaned up.

"You gonna miss your parents?" I ask.

"Sure, but I'm not disappearing forever. I'll call them tomorrow and tell them that you and I struck out on our own. They'll be worried, especially my dad. I feel bad about that. But they'll both get over it. At least I won't be sitting around their house mooching off them. I'll tell them we have a little money and that you know some people we can stay with in Little Rock."

"Why tell them that? I don't know nobody in Little Rock."

"They'll be upset. It'll make them feel better." He hugs the backpack close. "Besides, we have to go somewhere. I think we should go to Little Rock, or at least to Conway. With the cash we can get a prepaid credit card at Walmart and get a hotel room. Then in the morning we head down to Texas."

"So we're decided on Austin?"

"You put the thought in my head about Wally. I think it'd be cool for you to meet him."

"What kind of guy is he?"

"He's nice. You'll like him. I met him my second year at U of A, in a study group for this ridiculously hard lit class. The professor was this old lady who made us scan the meter of poems, and no one in the class could do it. So, a group of us got together to figure it out."

"Did y'all figure it out?"

"Not really. At least, I didn't. Wally and I became friends, though. He was the first openly gay guy I ever met, you know. He had a boyfriend named Harlan from back home in Texas. They'd been together since the tenth grade or something. I couldn't believe it. He didn't have any of the shit I had. I mean, he'd been through the usual stuff—rednecks calling him names, religious family members telling him that he was going to hell—but he just . . . didn't care. He just had—and I assume he still has—this perfect idea of himself. I always admired that about him. Can you imagine how tough you have to be to be gay in a place like Texas or Arkansas? Wally looks in the mirror, and he sees Wally, and he knows what that means. I look in the mirror, I just see this face. Sometimes it doesn't even seem like a person, just a face."

"You think too much."

I say it as a little joke, but he shrugs. "Maybe."

"We go to Austin, you know how to get in touch with him?"

"Oh, sure. I can text him tomorrow. I haven't talked to him in a while, but I know he'll be happy to hear from me."

"Think he'll like me?"

"What? Of course. Why would you ask that?"

"I'm just some ignorant-ass Ozark cracker. I've never been to college."

"Are you joking?"

"No."

"Wally doesn't give a shit about that. Believe me. If you like me, he'll like you."

I nod. I'm not sure that's true, but the idea of driving down to Texas and meeting new people is more exciting than scary.

Gary asks, "What about your mom?"

"What about her?"

"Will she be upset that you're leaving?"

I shrug. "One less problem for her to worry about. Won't have to listen to me fighting with Tommy."

Gary sits up. "And you don't think he's gonna be at the house, right?"

"Nah. Don't worry about that. He's up at the bar. He didn't go all the way up there just to turn around and come home. He'll be there 'til after closing time talking about that fucking statue."

"When's your mom get home?"

"She gets off work at midnight. Won't be home until one, unless she goes up to the bar to drink with Tommy." I look over at him. "Don't worry. We're almost done. We'll have the place to ourselves. You can take a shower. I need one myself. We'll pack up my shit. And then . . ."

He nods. "And then we go see Richard."

TWENTY-ONE BRIAN HARTEN

As we get into his truck, I ask Tommy, "We really gonna go up to his front door?"

"Not me. You."

I nod. "I got no problem with that."

"Damn right, you don't. You know where the preacher lives?"

"I think he lives over by the Closes. That's where they used to live, anyway. Ray's mom and stepdad used to live over there."

"I don't know where the Closes live."

"Just go up to School Hill. I can tell you where to turn."

As he drives, Tommy's all leaned back, his hand loose around the bottom of the truck's steering wheel, like he's barely thinking about the fact that he's driving. He shakes his head. "Jesus, you got yourself in a mess, Harten."

I just nod. Like I don't already know I shit the bed.

We come to a four-way stop, and a cop car pulls up behind us.

Tommy sits up, both hands on the wheel. Instead of going straight toward School Hill, he turns right.

He glances in the rearview mirror. The cop car turns after us.

"Shit."

"Think he's following us?"

"No reason he should be," Tommy says. We drive up to the turnoff and Tommy gets on the highway. The cop goes the other way.

"We'll come back around," he says. "Take the long way. I don't want the cops involved in this. Might not be a bad idea to wait 'til it gets a little darker, too."

I shrug, even though it's already dark outside. "Okay."

I figure he's still thinking about the cops or Weatherford, but then he says, "You should have asked me."

"For what?"

He just looks at me like I'm a dumb-ass.

"For money?" I say. "You won't even pay me what you owe me."

"First of all, I don't owe you shit. But I'm not even talking about money. I'm talking about the place itself. You should have asked me to go into business with you."

We're out on the highway, just a little north of town, and we pass by a big empty building overlooking a good view of the hills. The place has been four or five different restaurants in the last ten years. About every six months, somebody decides that they're the ones who can make this location work, so they spend a few months fixing up the place. Then they open. And then they close.

I say, "You telling me you would have gone into business with me?"

"Well," Tommy says, "I didn't know you then like I know you now. Now that I know you're a fucking moron, I wouldn't invest ten cents in any of your ideas. But you was a pretty decent employee when you worked for me. Gotta give you that. If you'd come to me and asked me to go in with you, yeah, I would have gave it real thought. I mean, I could have really helped you on that deal."

I don't say nothing to that, and he just gives me the side eye.

We ride along for a while, but he don't want to let it go. "You didn't even have the balls to come tell me you were going into business for yourself."

"I gotta tell you every move I make?"

He says, "Ain't about telling me every move you make. I never asked you about your business. But you trying to open a rival operation behind my back . . ."

"Rival operation? It's not like I'm trying to open Brian's Bar. I'm gonna open a liquor store. In another town, in another fucking county."

"Then why didn't you tell me what you were up to? Be honest now, Harten. You come into work every day and acted like nothing was up. I asked you every day, 'Hey, man, what's up? How you doing?' And every day you looked at me and smiled and you didn't say shit. Then I got to find out that you're talking to my distributors behind my back?"

"It wasn't anything personal, man. I was trying to start something for myself. That's all. It was just business."

"Fine, but you just remember that you're the one that made it all about money. You went behind my back, trying to open up a rival operation, and then today you steal from me? I mean, I treated you like a friend before you started all that shit."

I don't know what to say to that. I guess I did hide it from him. He's making it out like it was some big conspiracy, but it was more like I didn't want to fall on my ass in front of him. Plus, I guess there is a little something to the idea that I knew I would be his rival. If I'd been able to open my place, all the people from Van Buren County who drive over to Tommy's Bar would have stopped. They all would have come to my store.

God, it would have been great.

Tommy says, "Should've come to me, Harten."

"I get it, man. Lay off."

He's about to talk some more shit when the cab of his truck explodes in blue.

"Fuck me," he says.

"Cop behind us."

"You think?"

He slows down and pulls over to the side of the road and shuts off his engine. We're a few miles outside of Stock, on the downslope of the highway with the hills above us on the left and the valley below us on the right.

The cop pulls up behind us and leaves his blues on. Then he just sits there.

"Who is it?" I ask.

Tommy's looking in the rearview. "I can't tell."

The door opens on the cop car, and Tommy says, "Shit. It's the sheriff."

He rolls down his window and leaves his hands on the steering wheel.

"Just shut up and let me do the talking," he says.

I nod, but then it kind of hits me. He seems more nervous than I am, which is funny because as far as I know, I'm the only one here who's broken the law.

A flashlight sweeps the back window and creeps up the side of the truck. "Tommy," the sheriff says.

"Howdy, Bud," Tommy says.

I hear Bud say, "Who's that with you there?"

I give a little wave. "Hey, Bud. Brian Harten."

He comes up to the window and shines the light all over the inside of the cab. Bud's ex-military and looks it. He keeps his hair high and tight, and he's stayed in pretty good shape, considering he spends most of his day on his ass.

"What are you boys up to tonight?"

"Oh, not much."

"No? Where you heading?"

Tommy shrugs. "Nowhere particular."

"Heading nowhere particular pretty fast. You're doing seventy-eight in a fifty-five."

"Oh shit," Tommy says, looking at the dashboard, like the number might still be up there. "Just wasn't paying attention, I guess. I was telling Brian some old baseball stories. Got caught up in them, I guess. You remember the no-hitter I threw against Greenbrier?"

"No," Bud says, shining his light on the bench seat behind us. "But I never was much of a baseball fan. More of a football guy, myself."

You and everybody else in Arkansas.

Bud says, "Heard you had a little commotion tonight at the bar."

"Oh, yeah," Tommy says, raising his fingers off the steering wheel. "Had a fire. No one was hurt. Lost my statue, though."

"That's too bad. Know how it started?"

"Nope. Not yet. We got it all put out."

"Didn't have to call the fire department?"

"Naw. It was just the statue. Damn thing's all ruint, but there was no other damage to anything or anyone else. It was all over before anyone had time to grab a phone."

"No other problems?"

"Nope."

"Don't know how the fire started?"

"Nope."

"Sounds like arson."

"Oh, I doubt it. I figure some dumb-ass left a cigarette on it. Something like that."

"And no other problems?"

"Nope," Tommy says. "Everything's cool."

Bud shines the light on Tommy's hand resting on the steering wheel. "What happened to your knuckles?"

Tommy rubs his scraped knuckles like he's petting a kitten. "Nothing. Little altercation."

"About what?"

"Private matter."

Bud leans in and smiles a smile that's pure-bone meanness. "You telling me to mind my own business, Tommy?"

Tommy tries to laugh it off. "Course not." He kind of sighs and lifts his palms like it's all just so silly. "You know how I live with Carmen Fuller, right? Her girl Sarabeth lost her job today. I give her a hard time about it, and her boyfriend, that little weirdo Gary Doane, he swung on me. I defended myself. That's all."

"Gary okay?"

"Sure. He's fine. Just had to rake my knuckles on his head to calm him down. Nothing for anyone to get upset about. Everything's cool."

Bud looks back up the darkened mountain, his face going black and blue in the blinking lights from his car. He kind of mutters, "Everything is cool . . . ," and then he nods. "Okay, well, let me tell you what I know,

Tommy. Few hours ago, I get a call from Roy Taggart, the sheriff from over your ways. Tells me that there was a fire at your place. Says that by the time he got out there, you'd already been there and left. He talked to people at the scene, and the employees all said basically the same thing you just told me. But the *customers* at the scene were under the impression that the fire was set deliberately as some kind of diversion for a robbery. You know what I'm saying? The fire goes off, everybody runs out, someone runs in and hits the cash room. When the staff realize that the money is gone, they freak out and call you. You come up there and then, all the sudden, there's not any money missing and your boy Frankie James has changed his story."

"Who said all that? A couple of day drinkers? One of them was probably the one who left the cigarette on my statue."

"You're telling me there was no robbery?"

"Naw, man. If somebody stole from me, why wouldn't I call the cops?"

Bud looks at me. Then he looks back at Tommy's skinned knuckles. "I don't know, Tommy. Maybe you're a 'take the law into your own hands' kind of guy. Harten works for you. Maybe you boys got that bat in the back seat there because you're on your way to beat somebody's ass. You ain't out looking for Gary and Sarabeth, are you?"

Tommy just laughs at that and shakes his head. Gives me a 'can you believe this guy?' look. I try to laugh, but it just comes out like a little cough.

"Bud, c'mon, man. Gary and Sarabeth are a couple dumb-ass kids. They're harmless. And I got a baseball bat in the back because I love baseball. There's a ball and glove on the floor back there, too."

"And you're not on your way to mess up anybody else right now?"

Tommy says, "Course not."

Bud says, "Well, then, here's another theory off the top of my head. Maybe you didn't call the authorities because you didn't want to make it an official matter and have anyone getting within a country mile of your finances. Sheriff Taggart and I have both heard tell of some activities going on at both of your bars."

Tommy stops smiling, drops the friendly shit. "I don't know what you're talking about, Bud. I don't know who burnt down my statue or why. But I'm not on my way to beat nobody's ass, and I'm not hiding any illegal activity."

He keeps talking, protesting his innocence and all that, but I don't pay it much mind because I'm just now realizing that Bud has to be right. I wondered why Tommy didn't just call the cops on me from the start, and now I know. He wants to keep all this shit quiet.

"How about you, Brian?" Bud asks me. "You got anything to say?"

"No, Bud. Tommy's shooting you straight."

"Uh-huh." Bud nods. "I just want you both to think about what I said here tonight. Whatever's going on, you best watch yourselves."

We both say, "Yessir."

"And watch your speed," he tells Tommy.

Tommy gives him a little salute, and Bud struts back to his car.

Tommy starts the truck, and we pull away. Bud cuts his blues, but he pulls out behind us and stays there.

"He's following us," I say.

Tommy says, "Don't mean nothing. He's just heading back toward town."

"What are we gonna do if he keeps following us?"

Tommy thinks about that for a bit before he says, "We'll stop at Sonic."

"I think they might be closed."

"Then we'll stop at the Exxon and I'll get gas or something. Shut up and let me think."

I shut up and we ride for a while, and I guess he's thinking. I watch the trees go by in the dark. Behind us, the sheriff's car turns and goes down some road.

"The hell's he going?" I ask.

Tommy stares in the rearview. "Who cares? Long as he's gone."

I melt back into the seat. "Jesus."

He shakes his head, and I notice that he's sweating.

I say, "So what is it? Drugs? Girls?"

"The fuck you talking about?"

"Frankie James sells weed and crystal at both the bars. Everybody knows that. And I know that Sweetie and Katie are turning tricks. I bought a blow job off Sweetie myself."

"So, what's your point, Harten?"

"Bud was right. That's why you didn't call the cops."

He shrugs. "My business is my business. I don't need Taggart or Bud asking me a bunch of questions." He looks over at me. "Don't get the idea that changes things. It don't change shit. You still have to get me my goddamn money back."

"Yeah, I know."

"We're still heading to the preacher's house."

I lean forward. "Actually . . ."

"What?"

We're coming down the highway, and I point at the parking lot of the First Baptist Church, which is empty except for one minivan.

"He's still at work."

TWENTY-TWO RICHARD WEATHERFORD

They don't see me as they step into the sanctuary. Stopping by the back doors to take in the size of the auditorium, I hear Tommy Weller say, "Can't remember the last time I set foot in a church. Never been in this one. Big fucker, ain't it?"

"Please don't talk that way in my church," I say.

Weller laughs. "Where you at, Preacher?"

I've locked up the building except for the entrance that let them into the foyer. Most of the lights are off, just one spotlight from the balcony shining down on the microphone stand onstage, where tomorrow I'll narrate the Passion Play. I'm on the other side of the choir loft, in the shadows beneath Cody Crawford's cross.

I ease my way through the darkened set: a stone wall made of plastic, and a papier-mâché boulder in front of a tomb that's just brown felt draped over the skeleton of a family camping tent. I step gingerly so as not to disturb the handiwork of the Ladies' Auxiliary. Penny will know if a single detail is out of place in the morning.

I step into the light.

"Here," I say.

"What are you doing?" he asks.

"Tending to my business."

"Yeah?" he says, appearing at the steps of the stage with Brian Harten in tow. "Me too."

Brian stops by the pews.

Weller walks up the steps of the stage. He's carrying a baseball bat. There's a gun on his hip.

"Why do you have that?" I ask.

"I think you know."

"You brought a gun into my church to threaten me?"

He points the bat at me, and I can almost smell the sweat stains under the arms of his dirty pink polo shirt. "You got my money?"

I nod without acknowledging the bat or its implied threat. "Yes," I tell him. "You can have it back."

"Where is it?"

I take it from my back pocket and hold it out. He takes it, looking at me rather than at the money.

"How much is here?"

"All that I was given. I haven't touched it."

Over his shoulder, he asks, "How much, Harten?"

"Nineteen grand," Brian says. "And eight hundred."

Weller wedges the package of money into his back pocket and asks me, "So what the hell is this about?"

I shake my head. "What do you mean?"

"Why did this dipshit steal money from me and bring it to you? How come I got to come up to the Baptist church in the middle of the night to recover what was took from me?"

"I don't know how to answer that."

"How about you give it a shot?"

"I needed it."

"Why?"

"That's none of your business."

He shakes his head. "You made it my business when you sent this dumb-ass to my place to steal my money. Harten here burned down my statue." He points the bat at me. "That means *you* burned down my statue, and since this shithead ain't got no money, you're going to reimburse me."

"Okay," I say. "How much is that? How much do I owe you?"

"Five thousand dollars."

"Five thousand?"

"There's no way your stupid statue cost that much," Brian says.

Weller turns and points the bat down at Brian. Standing next to the front pew, just outside the glow of the spotlight hitting the stage, Brian looks pale and indistinct in the penumbra. Weller tells me, "You two guys owe me five thousand dollars. That's what I want."

Brian looks at me, scared.

I'm trying to think of how to answer him when Weller suddenly walks down the steps.

He stops beside Brian. Looking around, taking in the large sanctuary, with the high cathedral ceiling and the rows of pews, he says, "You know, all I got to do is tell people the truth when they ask what happened today. Brian Harten torched my statue and robbed my safe because the preacher put him up to it. And you know what everybody, including the cops, is gonna want to know? They're gonna want to know why Reverend Richard Weatherford, of all people, needed twenty grand so bad he'd enter into a criminal conspiracy to commit arson and robbery to get it." Weller turns to Brian and tells him, "I guess the preacher won't be throwing the dry vote your way, after all, Harten. All he talked you into was some jail time."

With that, Weller walks down the aisle and into the darkness, his shoes scratching against the carpet.

I hurry down the steps, past Brian, his face gone white and blank. "Mr. Weller?" I call out. "Tommy, wait. Let's talk about this."

I follow him into the foyer, a well of orange light shining in from the parking lot lamps. Our footsteps clack on the cheap linoleum.

"Please, wait, Tommy."

He reaches for the glass doors.

I grab his arm and pull him back. "Just wait a second and hear what—"

He yanks his arm away and raises the bat.

Palms raised, I circle around him and block the front door. My body is hot, and the glass is cool against my back.

"What are you doing?" he says. "Get out of the way."

"I can get you the five thousand."

"Price has gone up."

"What are you talking about?"

"Five thousand was the back-there price," he says. "Now we're at the 'I'm about to walk out the door' price."

"Which is what?"

"Why don't you tell me? But you better make it goddamn amazing because I'm about to walk out this door and get in my truck."

"Look, I don't have a lot of money laying around. But I do have a lot of money coming through this place every week. I could set some aside for you. I'm talking about a week-in and week-out, fifty-two-weeks-a-year revenue stream. Just take one minute and really think about that."

He doesn't say anything, so I keep going, scrambling for words, for ideas, to pull him in.

"There are other things besides the collection plate . . . The building fund, for instance. You're part owner of Arkansas Integrity Lumber, right? Right? So I talk the church into doing an addition, with Arkansas Integrity as our materials supplier. Plus, I could sweeten that deal for you, too, shave a piece off the top of the building fund for you? And what else? Events. Your pizza place is the new exclusive supplier of all our youth events from here on out. That's every Wednesday night and Sunday night . . ."

He laughs at the pizza thing, which is good, because at least I've got him talking to me.

"You bribing me with pizza money?"

"Here's what I'm saying. I'm saying you take a piece of the offering plate every Sunday. You take a piece of the youth group event fund every week. You take a piece of the building fund. You're pretty much part owner of the church at that point. That's for-sure money. Suing me? That's maybe money. Maybe you get it, maybe you don't, but it's less money and more hassle. And trashing my name around town? That won't put a single dollar in your pocket. But you do it my way, then you get a piece of everything this church does week-in and week-out for years to come. Are you really gonna walk out the door and leave all that money sitting here? Over a statue?"

Weller props the bat on his shoulder like a ballplayer casually taking in a view of the field before the game.

"How much does the church collect in a given week?" he asks.

"It depends on the time of year. After Easter and Christmas, there's always a spike."

Brian walks up behind Weller.

"You stick around," Weller tells him. "I ain't done with you yet."

Brian says nothing to that. Instead, he reaches out and pulls the gun from Weller's holster, points it at his back, and squeezes the trigger.

When the gun claps, we all jump. Weller drops the bat, and it rolls to my feet. He slips to one knee on the linoleum, the back of his shirt spotted black in the orange light. As he struggles to get up, he looks at me, cursing, his eyes as round as election buttons.

Brian holds a hand to one ear, and I realize that my own ears are ringing. He stares at Weller, down on one knee, like he's watching a child have an operation.

"Oh, Jesus," he says. "Tommy . . ."

"What the fuck, Brian," Tommy spits out with the last of his bluster. He feels his chest. There's no bullet hole. He tries to reach his back where the pain and blood is, but he can't. "What the fuck," he says again, but this time more in fear than anger. He looks at me. "Help me up."

I stare at him.

He's wobbly, feeling his chest as if he's having trouble breathing.

"Help me up, goddamn it," he says again, his rough voice cracking. Trying to sound reasonable, he says, "C'mon, now. I've been shot. We need to get me some help. Help me, now." He grabs my arm.

I look at Brian. "What did you do?"

His face is ashen and wet at the same time. He puts a hand to his forehead. "Jesus Christ. Jesus fucking Christ."

Weller gulps a breath and pulls at my arm. His thick, heavy hand is shaking and wet. "We need to call somebody." Then, realizing that he can do it himself, he reaches to his pocket for his cell phone.

"Tommy, stop," Brian says. He steps over to us and picks up the bat at my feet.

"Brian," I say.

Tommy Weller grabs my arm again, but I pull away from him and back up to the wall.

Weller fumbles for his phone, but Brian hits him in the face with the bat. I press harder against the wall. Weller falls over, crying and covering his head. Brian makes an ugly yelp, like he's just burned himself, and he swings the bat over his head like an ax, knocking a hole in the drop ceiling panel, and chops Weller on the back of the neck. Weller cries out, trying to cover his neck. Brian stops and stares at him, dust from the ceiling floating down on all of us, and then he takes a breath and grits his teeth and steps back into a swing, and this time he hammers a dent into the top of Weller's skull.

Lowering the bloody bat to his side, Brian just stares at him. We both do.

Weller reaches for his head—gently, slowly—but he's disoriented. He touches the cheap checkered linoleum instead. He caresses it with his fingertips.

TWENTY-THREE BRIAN HARTEN

Me and the preacher don't say a fucking word to each other. We just listen to Tommy breathe, and we stare at the gash in his skull. It looks like there's a bloody mouth that suddenly opened in the middle of his hair. I bend over and look at his eyes. Nothing. He takes a breath. I wait for him to let it out, but he doesn't.

My own heart is thumping. My ears are ringing. "Oh, Jesus." My eyes tear up, but Tommy's just stare out at nothing.

The preacher is looking at me, at the bat in my hand.

"I had to," I say. My voice cracks when I say it.

The preacher turns around and looks out the glass double doors of the church, at the little grassy slope between the empty parking lot and US-65.

That's when I realize I can see the highway from where I'm standing.

I didn't think. I didn't think about that at all.

I say, "No one drove past, right?"

The preacher stares out there without blinking. Then he shakes his head.

I drop the bat against Tommy.

The preacher's face is piss orange in the lamplight. I realize he's breathing harder than I am.

I wave at the doors. "Can people see in here?"

"I don't . . . I don't think so." He turns and looks at the doors. "Oh, God."

"You sure about that? Think. If anybody did drive past, could they see in here from the road?"

"I—I don't think so. At night, you can't see anything but the glare of the lights."

"Okay," I say. "Okay. Lock the doors." I wipe my tears away and bend down to grab Tommy's feet.

"What?"

"The doors, lock the doors."

He looks at them. He looks back at me. I think he's going to say something, but instead he steps over to the doors and locks them.

I take a deep breath. "We got to move him," I say.

The preacher looks at Tommy, the walls, the hole in the ceiling, the floor. He shuts his eyes. When he opens them, he says, "Let's get out of the way of the doors. Just in case."

I nod and take hold of Tommy's ankles. They're hairy and still wet with sweat. There's a men's room on one side of the foyer and a ladies' room on the other. I drag Tommy toward the ladies' room, smearing black blood across the floor. When I drop the feet, Tommy's lungs let go of his last breath. We both stop and stare at him until we're sure the fucker's not going to start moving.

My hands are slick with Tommy's sweat, and my gut feels like it's boiling. I try to think about what we should do next, but I can't think about anything except Tommy's sweat starting to dry on my palms.

The preacher says, "We need something to wrap him in, to contain the blood. We need to move him, but we need to wrap his head and chest, at least."

"Yeah . . ."

He says, "There's a clothes closet. Donations for the needy. We can get some of that and wrap him." He points at the big church hall. "It's through the sanctuary and—"

"You go get it," I say.

"You want to stay with the body?"

I don't want to stay with Tommy. And I don't want to be here alone if somebody with a key drives up.

"Where is it?" I say.

"Go through the sanctuary, go through the big double doors to the right of the stage. Go down the hall until you come to another set of double doors, go through those. The storage room is the first door on the right. Says 'Samaritan's Closet.'"

"What?"

"'Samaritan's Closet.' First door on the right."

I start to leave, but I stop at the door. "You . . . ain't gonna run off and leave me with a dead body, are you?"

"No. Are you?"

"No."

"Good. Do I look panicked to you, Brian?"

Actually, he doesn't, not anymore. He looks like the same guy who's been kicking my ass at county board meetings for the last few months.

"No."

"Then go get the clothes. I don't think there are towels, but there will be sweaters and shirts, things like that. Get something to wrap around his head and put over his back. Hurry now."

I hurry through the big church hall. It's spooky, quiet and dark, with the spotlight hitting the stage next to a big cross. I'm walking up the aisle in the dark—*i was eight years old, my mom was sick and my aunt took me to this church to pray for her, and i prayed, and the old preacher said step out from the aisle if you want to be saved from hell, and i stepped out and walked up here and asked him to pray for me and my mom, and he said he would, but he said do you want to be saved, and i asked do i need to, and he said yes but not today, today i can just pray for you and your momma, and i said thank you*—and I get to the double doors and go through. The place is dark, but since some of the windows are visible from the highway, I don't want to turn on any lights. I take out my cell. The cracked screen still glows, and I use the light to creep down the hallway. Crooked shadows bounce over the walls with every step I take.

The office door on the left reads, "Richard Weatherford, Senior Pastor." Door on the right reads, "Prayer Room." Then a men's restroom. Drinking fountain. Women's restroom. Farther down, a door on the left reads, "Church Secretary." Taped to the wall is a poster of a baby sleeping in an American flag slung from a cross. Then a door that reads, "Dustin Fields, Youth Pastor."

I come to some double doors. Aluminum with little windows. I peek through and see another long creepy hallway. I open one of the doors. On the right is a wooden door with a plate that reads, SAMARITAN'S CLOSET.

I open it up. It's a closet with big plastic storage tubs sitting on shelves with labels scribbled in Sharpie on pieces of masking tape. *Boys Shirts, Girls Shirts, Boys Pants, Girls Pants, Baby Clothes.* There's a bunch of them. I find one marked *Sweaters* and pull out a couple of neatly folded sweaters. In a tub marked *Misc*, I find a black housecoat with no belt.

I get my stack of stuff and hurry back through the double doors, and I'm a couple of steps down the hall when they slam shut behind me. I yelp like a dog and drop the phone. It lands facedown, and I have to get on the carpet on my knees and feel around for it in the dark. When I find it, I swing the light back at the door. I just stare at it until I'm sure nothing else is going to happen.

TWENTY-FOUR RICHARD WEATHERFORD

There was a moment—I saw it in his eyes—when he realized that we were going to kill him. Tommy looked up at me, and his eyes clearly asked me, *Are you going to let this happen?* And I know he saw *Yes* on my face. Before that moment, it never occurred to him that Brian and I valued our circumstances more than we valued his life.

It never occurred to me, either.

Now, the reality of the peril I'm in has scrubbed my mind clean. I'm aware of what must happen next, and I'm aware of the danger that this corpse poses to me. The prospect of discovery sends an electrical charge across my flesh and clarifies my thinking. I'm scared, but I'm not panicked. I know, with simple clarity, that these are the most dangerous hours I have ever lived.

Perspiration covers me like a new layer of skin. My body is manifest. My breath and my bowels and my blood. I am alive. Despite the danger I'm in—no, *because* of it—I've never felt my own living so intensely. I've always thought of the body as a humiliating trap of disease and pain, but now at last, at last, I realize that I am nothing but a body.

My senses are raised. I'm overwhelmed by the odors of cleaning agents and blood and sweat. The silence of the church is punctuated by my own breathing and the whispers and creaks of the building itself.

Until this moment, I have lived my life in the future, in dreams and fears and hopes and anxieties. I've lived in preparation for tomorrow, and for next year, and for eternity itself.

Standing over this dead man, however, I realize how wrong I've been. I stare at his curled hand, and then at my own hand. We are meat for the slaughterhouse floor.

TWENTY-FIVE BRIAN HARTEN

He's standing right where I left him, and he's staring at his hand like a fucking idiot.

And there's Tommy dead on the floor—*tommy at the bar cracking peanuts with one hand dropping the shells with his pinkie and flicking the nuts in his mouth with his thumb, tommy laughing so hard he wipes tears away*—and I have to piss so bad. The door of the ladies' room is open, and I drop the clothes and push through it and barely get my dick out in time. The piss runs out of me, and I'm light-headed.

When I flush and come out of the bathroom, the preacher's leaning over Tommy, wrapping the robe around his torso.

"I don't know, man," I say.

He yanks at the robe. "There was no belt for this robe?"

"No."

"That's too bad. It would help to secure it around him."

"I said I don't know about this, man."

"What don't you know?"

"About this. I fucking killed him. I fucking killed Tommy. I mean . . ."

He nods like he's heard this before, like it's all a part of being a preacher. "You stepped away for a few minutes," he explains, "occupying your mind and your attention with a task. Now that you've stepped back into this room, you're shocked by the reality of it all. That's understandable. But nothing's changed from the moment you stepped out of the room. It hasn't gotten better, and it hasn't gotten worse. Nothing's changed. We still have to deal with it."

He pulls a T-shirt from the pile and wraps it around Tommy's head like a bag, tying the bottom. He stares at it a second, stands up and goes into the bathroom, opens the little cabinet door under the sink, and fishes out a box of small plastic trash bags. He walks back over to Tommy, kneels, and using a couple of bags as gloves, starts to slip a third bag over Tommy's wrapped head.

Seeing his head all wrapped that way, I can't breathe. I have to gasp for air.

The preacher glances up at me and nods to himself. His voice is calm. "Don't look at this. Look at the wall. Good. Take a breath. Maybe you'd feel better if we discussed our plan."

I catch a breath and let go of it slowly. Then I say, "We don't have a plan."

"Well, then, let's develop a plan."

"What do we do, man? I don't know . . ."

"It depends on what we want to happen next. If the police find him here, then our lives are over. Your life as you know it is over."

"Jesus fucking Christ."

"Yes. Exactly. Jesus fucking Christ." He nods. "I always wondered what the appeal of blasphemy was. Now I get it. It's a way of dragging the Almighty down to our level."

"What the fuck are you talking about?"

He waves that away. "Here's the point, Brian. Unless you want to go to jail tonight, we need to get rid of this body."

"But we can't just dump him down the road somewhere."

"No, we can't. So, let's think. How did you two get here? Together?"

"Yeah. In his truck."

He thinks about it. "Where is it?"

"Parked on the side."

"Under the trees?"

"Yeah."

"Good. That's good. It's a well-shaded spot, and it's not visible from the north side of 65. That means that only people coming from the south could see it, and I think they'd have to really be looking. So, there's a good chance, especially at this time of night, that no one even saw you."

I take a breath and look down. He's got the shirt wrapped around Tommy's crushed head to soak up the blood and then the bag around that to catch any spillage. He ties the bag at Tommy's neck. And it kind of hits me again. Tommy is dead. I've known him for years, and he's dead on the floor. "I killed him . . ."

"It was self-defense. Like you said, you had to do it. If we had let him hold this thing over us, then what?"

"I . . . killed him."

"We both did. That's what a jury would say."

"Jesus." I rub my face, and my hand drips with sweat. "I just knew that no matter what else happened between the two of you, I'd be fucked. I'd lose the store, my kids, probably go to jail."

The preacher stops what he's doing and looks at me.

I say, "Now, though—now I just think we're fucked."

"Don't talk that way. We can still make this work."

"No, man. Look, I think—"

"Stop it, Brian," he says. "Don't even say it. We all had our chance to do the right thing, and none of us took it. Me, you, and Tommy. All of us. That chance is gone, and now we're managing the consequences. You really want to go to jail? What will happen to your kids?"

My face gets hot. "Don't talk about my kids, man. You don't give a shit about me or my kids."

"I don't matter, Brian." Still using the bags as gloves, he pulls off Tommy's belt and uses it to fasten the robe tight around his bloody torso. "Don't think about me at all. I don't care about you, and you don't care about me. Fine. So forget about me. Ask yourself what's going to happen to you, and then make your decision based on that. That's what I'm going to do."

"What does that mean?"

He looks up and kind of takes in the whole church. "It means I'm not going to throw away my life tonight. Neither should you. We can still make this work."

"I don't know what you're saying, man. Tommy is dead. We can't make that go away."

"Yes, we can. I can."

"How?"

"We put his body in his truck, and we take him to the bridge."

"Oh, Jesus."

"And we throw him over."

"Jesus fucking Christ, man. Then we go to jail. Anyone can tell he was murdered."

"Yes, but it can be made to look like someone else did it."

"Who?"

"Gary Doane and Sarabeth Simmons."

"Tommy's stepdaughter, or whatever?"

"Yes, that's the one. And her boyfriend."

"Gary Doane is the kid who went crazy . . ."

"Exactly. Everyone knows that he's got emotional issues. And she's nothing but a slut."

"But why frame them?"

"Because the money is for them."

"The money . . . is for them . . . Why?"

The preacher takes a deep breath. "Because I've been sleeping with Sarabeth. They were blackmailing me."

"Oh, Jesus, man."

"You'll have to help me carry the body out to the truck. It's perfect. We dump the body, and then I pay off Gary and Sarabeth and they skip town with the money. You think that won't make them the prime suspects?"

"Yeah, it would, but they'll say you gave them the money. They'll say you gave it to them."

He shrugs. He's so calm now he can fucking shrug. "And I'll say I didn't."

"I don't know, man."

He shakes his head. "But *I* know, Brian. You're going to help me dump Tommy over the bridge, and then you're going to go home, and nothing bad is going to happen to you. If the police come and talk to me, I'll handle it."

"Am I supposed to just take your fucking word for that?"

"The other option is to call the police and go to jail. We can go home tonight, or we can go to jail tonight. I know what my choice is."

I try to think about it, but it's too hard. He's acting so cool. He stands up. You wouldn't know that he was standing over a dead guy. He's calm, and it's weird, but that makes me feel a little better. It's like we're both lost, but at least he has some idea of where to go.

But what about Bud?

"The sheriff seen me with Tommy," I tell him.

"When?"

"Tonight. Like a hour ago."

"Did you talk to him?"

"Yeah."

"What'd you tell him?"

"Nothing, really. But I could tell he thought we was out looking for the money."

"He know you were coming to see me?"

"No."

"Good. Then if they ask you what happened, you say Tommy dropped you off at the church. And I'll back you up. You came to the church, and we discussed the vote, and Tommy left to find Gary and Sarabeth."

That makes sense. I could do that. Me and the preacher were talking at the church, and Tommy run off and went after the kids who stole from him.

The preacher says, "It's good. This will work. You and I have an alibi. Tommy dropped you off. And I saw him drive off. I'm a perfect alibi for you, and you're a good alibi for me."

I don't know what else to do. I nod.

The preacher looks at me like he understands, like he's my dad talking me through a hard time. "This will be over soon," he says.

"I just—"

"It's going to be okay, Brian. Nothing can bring Tommy back. So we have to think about what's best for us and what's best for our families. We can do this."

"Yeah . . ."

"We can iron out the details later, but right now, we need to do this. Right?"

"Right. Yes."

I bend down slowly and pull up Tommy's socks, because I don't want to touch his bare legs. Solid. He feels weird and solid. His socks are still sweaty. The preacher gets him under the arms and we lift him up. Heavy. We grunt. I gag, because Tommy is dripping piss and shit inside that robe. The preacher grunts.

"Hold on a sec," the preacher says, and we put Tommy down. The preacher scans the highway and unlocks the door.

"The truck is in the side lot?"

"Yes."

"Good. Once we get to the truck, the trees and the shade make it less likely that someone can see us from the road. So, the only thing we have to worry about is the short space between here and the truck."

I nod.

He scans the highway again.

"This is it," he says. "We go hard and fast."

"Okay."

He unlocks the door and opens it and we're outside. The air is cold, and Tommy is heavy, and I need to piss again. My hands are sweaty, and my legs are burning, and I'm scared I'm going to drop him. *What are we doing?* We carry him across the parking lot and into the shadows beneath the pines and lay him on the ground. While the preacher digs through Tommy's pockets for his keys, I catch my breath. The preacher puts the keys in his own shirt pocket and drops the tailgate. Then we grunt and heave Tommy into the bed of the truck.

"The bat," the preacher says. He looks at me hard for a minute and finally says, "I'll be right back." Then he runs back into the church.

And now I'm alone, standing by the truck in the shadows, and Tommy is dead, and the grasshoppers and crickets are so loud tonight, it's like they're yelling at me.

now's your chance to leave

Can't. Nowhere to go. Gotta do what's best for me. For the kids.

I look up at the church. It's so big. If he runs something this big, he's gotta know what he's doing.

He comes out with the bat and tosses it in the back of the truck, and it thuds against Tommy. He climbs into the truck bed and undoes the robe, pulls Tommy's arms out of the sleeves, and unties the bag and all the stuff on Tommy's head. Then he puts the belt back on Tommy, with the empty holster on his hip. "I'll dispose of this stuff," he says, waving at the robe and the bag. "He has to go into the water in nothing but his own clothes."

I nod.

"Get in," he says, climbing out of the bed.

He's so calm. I can barely think straight, and he's so fucking calm.

I get in the passenger side, and he slides in the driver's side and starts the ignition. We pull out and creep down the service road.

At the end of the road, where it turns onto the highway, there's a little grove of trees I've never noticed before, and he pulls in there and shuts off the truck. I look through the back window, and Tommy is laying there in moonlight, clear as day.

"Anybody can see him."

"No one will," the preacher says.

TWENTY-SIX RICHARD WEATHERFORD

From where we're parked in the trees, we can see the highway as it descends the hill and passes the church, crosses the bridge, and then skirts the edge of downtown, headed north. A truck tops the hill coming our way. At the same time, distant headlights approach from town.

"Okay," I say. "After this car and truck pass, we go. We have to do this quickly. We don't want to be on the bridge any longer than we have to be. So, once I throw the truck in park, we jump out, grab him, and over he goes."

I glance at Brian to see if he understands. He's staring at me.

"What?" I ask.

He shakes his head. "I can't believe this is you."

I turn my attention back to the highway. The truck speeds down the hill and passes the car coming across the bridge. The taillights of the truck fade in darkness. The car climbs up the hill.

"I'm not myself right now," I tell him.

He seems to accept that as an answer but says, "Then who are you?"

I almost laugh at that.

"So," he says, "it was all just bullshit?"

"What?"

"Your whole Christian thing. This whole time. Everything that everybody thinks about you. It's just an act? *This* is the real you?"

"Get ready," I say. The car disappears over the hill in a whisper, and I turn the ignition and hit the gas.

TWENTY-SEVEN BRIAN HARTEN

The truck lunges forward in the dark. I want to close my eyes, but I can't. Without headlights, the night is as blue as a bruise and it's like I'm being pushed from behind. The black highway and trees and the bridge and water.

At the middle of the bridge, the preacher hits the brakes. He swings right up to the railing, so close I have to squeeze out. I've driven across this bridge a million times, but I've never stood on it. In the dark, it feels like we're a mile up from the beating water. We run around to the back, drop the tailgate, and each grab a leg. I look over my shoulder. No cars coming. We drag Tommy out of the truck bed, hoist him up, and flop him against the railing. Then we lift him up and over and he drops away from us. One shoe flies off in the dark. I can make out his pink shirt as he plops into the river.

The water takes his body, and it disappears beneath the bridge, and the back of my head explodes

crack

no, i try to yell, stop

crack crack

rail

over

air

scream can't

water flies up

n

TWENTY-EIGHT RICHARD WEATHERFORD

I wipe off the bloody bat with the robe and throw it over the bridge after Brian. Then I toss the robe into the truck bed and run to the open door. I have to do a three-point turn to get the truck pointed back toward the church. As I do, the gun, the money, and Weller's cell phone all slide off the seat and clatter on the floorboard. No cars pass as I race back to the service road.

I'm winded when I jump out of the truck and pause to catch my breath. I survey the parking lot. No vehicles except my own.

I collect the stuff from the floorboard and run into the church and lock all the doors behind me. I should be alone. No one with a key has cause to come here this late. I check my phone. No new messages.

Blood in the foyer.

I grab liquid hand soap from the foyer bathroom and hurry through the darkened sanctuary. Passing the organ flanking the right of the stage, I go into the baptistery dressing room and recoil at my image in the mirror. The dried blood of Tommy Weller and Brian Harten dots my skin like freckles. Stripping naked, I collect some towels and climb the stairs to the baptistery. I run the water warm and use the soap to wash myself. Then I use the towels to wash the baptistery. The blood washes off easily.

I know, of course, that there is no way for me to clean up all the microscopic evidence of my crimes, and it would be a waste of time for me to attempt to do so. It is better to clean myself, to clean the scene, and to hope that the deaths of Weller and Harten do not lead the police here. My greatest bulwark, I remind myself, is that no one has a reason to suspect me. No one has a reason to come here and look for evidence of murder, here of all places.

After I've cleaned myself thoroughly, I retrieve a dry towel and wrap it around my waist. I hurry to the janitor's closet, grab the fiberglass cleaner and a black garbage bag, and take it all back to the foyer. The towel keeps coming loose, so I slip it off while I clean the foyer from top to bottom. I wash the windows, scrub the floors on my hands and knees, wipe down the walls and the doors. I take out the damaged ceiling tile and carry it downstairs to the dumpster. I break it up into four pieces before I dispose of it. On my way back up, I grab a replacement from the basement supply closet. I fix the ceiling, then turn on the lights in the foyer so that I can inspect everything. When I'm content that all looks normal, I shut off the light.

Then I bathe myself again, dry myself off, throw everything into the bag, and go to my office. I keep a spare pair of clothes in my office to wear under my robe when I baptize new believers. It's just a plain gray T-shirt, jeans, underwear, and socks that I keep in my coat closet. I get dressed and take the garbage bag downstairs to the other janitor's closet, where we have the washer and dryer. They were gifts from the estate of elderly Sister Rutherford a couple of years ago. She worried about people having to tote home wet clothes after being baptized. Odd, the things people care about. The truth is we don't have enough baptisms to justify such a thing, but it's nice to have the washer and dryer here for towels and table linens. During the last bad tornado season, we were able to help out several families who lost their power.

We have a bottle of Tide Ultra, which Penny bought for the express purpose of washing the fake blood out of the Easter costumes. I soak my clothes, the towels, and the clothing I wrapped around Tommy.

Then I start the washer. I don't know if the stains will come out completely, but either way, this will make them less obvious. When everything is washed and dried, I'll fold it all neatly at the bottom of my office closet until I can bag it up and throw it in the dumpster just before the trash pickup on Monday.

I run upstairs and look over everything once more. I turn on all the lights and look for spots on the floors of the sanctuary and the hallways, but I don't see anything. Still, I make a note to call the carpet cleaners on Monday.

I climb the baptistery steps, look everything over, and turn off the lights in the dressing room. I walk back up to the sanctuary and check the Easter stage.

Everything is in order.

Scrolling through the contacts on Tommy's phone, I find her. Sarabeth Simmons.

I look at his last few texts to get a feel for how he writes. The hallmarks of his style seem to be all caps, an inability to distinguish between *its* and *it's*, and no use of punctuation outside of an abuse of the exclamation point.

I sit down on the front pew beside Tommy's gun.

I text her.

TWENTY-NINE SARABETH SIMMONS

I'm packing my final bag when my phone dings. It makes me jump. Even though they don't have my number, I'm afraid it might be Gary's parents. I pull it out and read it.

"What the hell?"

"What?" Gary asks, drying his hair with a towel.

I show it to him. "Look at this shit."

It's from Tommy. I NEED TO TALK TO YOU

Gary frowns. "What does he want?"

"I have no idea. Maybe he doesn't want me to tell my mom about what happened? I wouldn't be surprised if he wanted me to be quiet about it. God, what a piece of shit."

I write him back, After what u did? Go fuck urself

A second later he texts, ITS IMPORTANT!

I fire back, U goin and fuckin urself is important

That one slows him down, but after a minute or so he writes, ITS ABOUT THE MONEY

"He said what?" Gary asks.

I show him.

We stare at each other for a second.

"What's he mean?" I ask.

Gary sits down on my bed. His skin is still pink from the shower. "He doesn't mean the money from the preacher. He doesn't know about that."

"No."

"Ask him what he's talking about."

What money? I text.

I almost shit when he writes back, **YOU KNOW WHAT MONEY**

Gary says, "He has to mean about the money we're getting from the preacher."

"But he don't know anything about that."

"You sure? You didn't let something slip out?"

"No, of course not. I'm not a complete idiot. I didn't tell anybody. And if I was going to tell somebody, I wouldn't tell him. Are you sure you didn't tell anybody?"

"No, of c—"

The phone dings again. Tommy got tired of waiting. **U KNOW WHAT MONEY! THE MONEY U AND GARY THOUGHT U MADE TODAY! LETS MEET!!**

"Shit," Gary cusses. "He knows."

"I don't understand how he could know about it."

"Doesn't matter now. What's he going to do? He wouldn't care, right?"

"Well, he wouldn't try to stop us from doing it, but he damn sure would try to get some for himself."

Gary just stares at me. "Really?"

"What do you think we should do? He wants to meet."

Gary shakes his head. "I don't want to."

I can tell he's afraid of getting beat up again, but I'm more afraid of Tommy getting pissed and fucking up this whole thing for us. If he starts talking about it to people, then it could go really bad. "Gary, if he knows, then we gotta talk to him. Like you said, we're into illegal shit here. They put people in jail for what we're doing. He ain't gonna say anything texting or over the phone, and I don't think we should, either. So, let's meet him and see what he knows."

He nods. "Okay."

"Okay?"

"Yeah, okay. Let's see where he wants to meet."

THIRTY GARY DOANE

I leave the keys to my mom's car in the ignition, grab my bag, and run back to Sarabeth's car. I don't have to run, though. I know they're in still in bed. As Sarabeth eases us down the sleepy street I grew up on, I look back at my house, dark and quiet except for the front porch light that my father left on for me. I take Sarabeth's hand.

We say nothing as she drives back toward town. She doesn't turn on the radio, so we sit in silence, holding hands, listening to the wind whistle over the car.

Everything feels different. In some ways, it's like we've been playing around before today. I'm in awe of this new feeling. I love her. She loves me. I've never felt closer to someone than I do to her in this moment. I know I can rely on her, and she knows she can rely on me. What an extraordinary thing, so simple, but it feels solid and real, concrete beneath my feet.

What did I think we were doing before now? So much of our relationship has been based on shared resentments. We hated all the same people. When we first started discussing Richard, I was surprised how much anger boiled up from both of us. What had he actually done to us at that point? Nothing, really. He'd mostly presided over the town's hypocrisy. He'd blessed the lies the people here tell themselves. He told them that they were good, decent Christians, no matter how petty and small their lives were. We hated him for it.

We hated the town, we wanted to get away from our parents, and we wanted to wake up somewhere different. We shared all of that.

But I didn't know I loved her until now.

Was she just using me? At first, sure. Sarabeth has been through a lot. It's been bad for me here, but I know it's been worse for her. My parents aren't perfect, but I do know they love me. What has Sarabeth had? An indifferent mother who's lived with a series of drunks and creeps. Sarabeth did what she had to do to survive. But things have changed now. She loves me, and I love her.

So now this is it. I need to be strong for her. I need her to be strong for me. We're leaving town tonight, and that's that. We'll call the preacher. Either he gives me all my money tonight, or he gives us enough to get on the road. He can send us the rest in monthly installments. That was Sarabeth's idea. Smart.

First, though, we have to see Tommy one last time. We have to figure out what he knows. If he starts something, we'll deal with it and we'll deal with it together.

I look over at her.

She doesn't notice me for a while. She's focused on the road, focused on where we're going. When she does finally catch me gawking at her, she says, "What?"

"I love you, Sarabeth."

She smiles, gives my hand a little shake. She looks over at me. "Yeah?"

"Yeah."

She shakes her head. "That amazes me," she says. She squeezes my hand. "It really does."

I smile at her.

She puts both hands back on the wheel. The dashboard glows in her glassy eyes. "Don't get me crying now," she says with a chuckle. "Save it for later."

THIRTY-ONE SARABETH SIMMONS

When I come to the bridge, I turn onto the skinny dirt road going down to the river where Tommy wants to meet us. Gary's knee starts bouncing like it always does when he's nervous. I rest a hand on his leg, and he smiles and nods. The road curves around the hill, blotting out the moon on my side, but through Gary's window I can see the light skipping across the water. When I get to the bend, headlights leap out of the dark at us.

I swerve to miss the truck, but when I do the road disappears. I scream. I can't move, can't take my foot off the gas. Gary reaches for the wheel, but we're already racing headfirst down the hill. Saplings snap against our headlights and pine branches slap the windshield. We hit a tree, but we don't stop. We're going too fast. The tree bends, grinding under the driver's-side wheel, and we flip.

Now is motion and iridescent light and impact and glass bursts in my face and we slam to a stop.

I close my eyes to stop the spinning. I taste wet dirt. I hear the untroubled river rushing by. When I open my eyes, Gary is half out of the car and half in it, and I try to scream, but I can't get a breath.

A man walks up to the car.

The preacher.

He stares. He looks frightened. I try to beg him for help, but my mouth is nothing but blood and dirt and glass.

He walks over to Gary and leans into the car.

i try to speak to him

no breath
mosquito wings screaming in my ear
blood pooling in my eyes
no breath
i cant hear the river
cant hear the mosquito
moonlight turns red
then black

THIRTY-TWO RICHARD WEATHERFORD

I creep up my front steps as silently as a thief, but I'm shaking so badly I have to stop before I reach the door and grip the railing. I don't know if it's nerves or exhaustion. I just want to collapse on my bed and pass out, but I'm not sure I can. At this moment, it doesn't feel like I'll ever be able to get to sleep.

I close my eyes and wait for a wave of dizziness to pass.

When I'm ready, I dig my keys out of my pocket. I turn the knob on the front door as carefully as the lock on a safe. As I'm easing the door closed behind me, I realize that Penny is sitting on the living room couch.

She stares at me in the weak glow of a single end table lamp. Even the stairwell light, which we always leave on at night, has been shut off. There's no illumination from upstairs, where our children are sleeping, lost in their own particular dreams or nightmares.

Penny's hands rest on her thighs, her bare feet flat on the floor. She waits for me to speak.

Quietly I ask, "What are you still doing up?"

She stands. She hasn't dressed for bed and is wearing the same jeans and charcoal jumper she's been wearing all day. "Come here, Richard," she says.

She leads me to the hallway and opens the basement door. Turning on the light, she starts down the stairs. "Close the door," she says.

I do, and follow her down the wooden steps. At the bottom, she turns around. Looking small between large boxes stacked to the ceiling, she crosses her arms.

"Tell me."

"What?"

She shakes her head as if to say *what* isn't good enough anymore. "Tell me, Richard. Just tell me. Just say the words out loud. Do me the favor, after all these years, of just saying the words out loud."

I have to plant my feet and steady myself before I can manage to say, "Okay."

"You've been cheating on me."

"Yes."

Her mouth tight, she nods. Swallows.

"That's not it, though, is it?" she asks. "That's only part of it."

"Yes."

"Tell me the rest."

There's a faint ringing in my right ear and the thrum of blood in my temples. The muscles between my shoulders are knotted tight. I can't bring myself to lie to her. I'm too exhausted, too emotionally wrung. The entire day is catching up with me. And she doesn't blink. She's demanded the truth, and there's no longer any way to keep it from her.

I take a breath and say, "I've put all of us in danger."

She just stares at me, her mouth grim. The only evidence of feeling in her is the breath she takes before she says, "What did you do?" She looks closer at my face, my clothes, my hands. "Just tell me."

I nod, but I still don't know how to come out and tell her what I've done.

She says, "Who did you see this morning?"

I take a breath and let it out slowly.

"Gary Doane."

Her expression doesn't change. Her eyes shift as she looks from one of my eyes to the other. Then she shuts her eyes for a moment. She nods to a thought she doesn't vocalize.

"Tell me the rest," she says. "Tell me all of it. Don't make me drag it out of you."

I tell her. I'll tell her all of it, God help me. I don't try to spin the story. I just tell her, starting with Gary's phone call this morning, what happened.

At first, her expression hardens into cold fury. She stares at me, her jaw clenched, her arms crossed low, like she's holding her stomach. I walked in the door tonight as her husband and the next moment I became a homosexual and an adulterer. Now I'm also a crooked preacher playing backroom politics with Brian Harten. But I can't stop for her to take it in. I don't have hours and hours for a conversation about adultery. The wreck was visible from the bridge. Police are probably already there. I need to get her past the merely painful to the truly horrific.

"Brian stole the money from Tommy Weller," I tell her. "When Weller found out it was Brian, he confronted both of us."

Her face is white, but her voice is steady as she asks, "What happened?"

"Brian killed Tommy."

Her mouth opens.

"And then," I say, tears filling my eyes, "in self-defense, I killed Brian." Even as my voice is breaking on those words, I'm surprised by this surge of emotion, as if there is a part of me forever observing my own feelings like the distant movements of clouds.

Her right hand rises to her mouth. Her gaze drops to my clothes.

"You're telling me the truth?" she says.

I nod. I clear my throat softly. "Yes," I say. "I'm sorry. I am so sorry, Penny."

"What about Gary? Where is he right now?"

"He died, too. He and Sarabeth both. They . . . they ran off the road."

"Richard . . ." She presses her hand harder against her mouth and stares at the concrete floor.

For a time, she doesn't speak. I stand there with nothing to say, nothing to do but wait, amid the wreckage of our marriage, of our family, and wonder what she will do.

What will I let her do? Isn't that the real question? Will I let her strike me again or curse me or run past me and wake the children and flee our home before the roof caves in? Will I really let her do that? After all I've done tonight, can I really let her call the police?

As I watch my wife weigh her options, I have a terrible vision. A vision of murder, in this cold and quiet basement, at this dark hour, while my children sleep upstairs. A few days ago, I would have been horrified to have such a vision. I would have believed that such a thing was impossible. This day, however, has relieved me of my mistaken belief that anything like the impossible exists when it comes to human beings. Until today, I've shut my eyes and stopped up my ears to the truth the world has been howling at me my whole life. All the people I've known, all the tragedies, large and small, that I've witnessed—none of it got through to me. I refused to see, refused to listen. I barricaded myself behind walls of Scripture and doctrine. I hid behind the veneer of my own reputation, hidden even—perhaps especially—from myself.

The things I've done tonight have taught me another truth. I'm just a human being, and human beings are capable of anything.

Yet even as I know this, I also know there's nothing to be gained by an act of violence committed in this house. I need Penny. If something were to happen to her, it would only make my unmasking by the police inevitable.

There's something else, too. She hasn't run out of the house yet. She's still here. And when she looks away from me and stares up at a blank space on the ceiling, I realize she is staring in the direction of the children's rooms. Yes, I'm capable of anything. But then again, so is she.

"I should call the police," she says.

I nod. "Perhaps you should."

"You think I won't?"

"I think you'll do whatever is best for the children."

"Of course, I'm going to do what's best for the children."

"Of course."

"Is that all you can say? 'Of course'?"

"I can tell you why you shouldn't call the police."

"Why?"

"Because this is almost over. Because everything that's happened tonight will be attributed to the actions of other people. Because everybody who died tonight died as the result of choices they made. I'm the only person involved who has no obvious connection to any of this. If we do nothing, if we act normal, we're safe."

For the first time, she looks like she might cry. "Safe? That's not the point. What about Gary? Or his parents?"

"He set out to seduce me so that he and that girl could blackmail me. I'm sorry about what happened to Gary, but he wasn't an innocent victim in any of this. Neither of them was. You have to understand that."

"That doesn't make it okay."

"There's no *okay*. There's just what is. If I go to jail tonight, it won't bring anyone back to life. It won't relieve anyone's suffering. It will only hurt our children."

She stares at me. "You'd use our children to protect yourself . . ."

I shake my head. "I'm not using them. I don't care about myself anymore. When I threw Brian Harten off that bridge, a part of me went into the water with him. I deserve to go to jail for what I did tonight. I know that. And if you need to call the police, then I'll understand. You want to do the right thing. But if I go to jail, it's going to traumatize our children for the rest of their lives. They'll all have to pay for my sins."

She closes her eyes. "God help me." She holds up a hand. "Just . . . shut up." Finally, she opens her eyes. "How do you know the police aren't on their way here?"

"Because I'm not personally connected," I say. "Gary and Sarabeth, Brian and Tommy—they're all connected. I'm just Gary's pastor. There's nothing to connect me."

"Texts and voicemails with Gary?"

"Just a handful. Nothing that wouldn't seem professional, just a pastor talking to a troubled member of his congregation."

"And no one else knows about you and Gary?"

"No."

"Are you sure?"

"As far as I know."

"As far as you know?"

"Yes. I have no reason to think Gary and Sarabeth would have told anyone else about their blackmail scheme. And I have every reason to think they would have kept it a secret."

Gradually her gaze drifts to the floor. She shakes her head and runs her fingers through her hair, down her scalp, until she's clutching the back of her neck. Her face is blank, slack, lost in thought, until something occurs to her and she looks at me.

"What happened to the money?"

The question takes me off guard. "The money? It's with Gary and Sarabeth."

She stares at me. "You said they ran off the road."

"They . . ."

"You ran them off the road."

I chew the inside of my cheek for a moment before I say, "Yes. It was the last piece. For them to take the responsibility for what happened . . ."

"They couldn't be around to tell the truth," she says.

I say nothing to that.

She says, "And then you threw the money inside the car."

"Yes."

She closes her eyes. I wait for her. She looks like she's in pain when she finally says, "Are you sure you didn't leave any footprints?"

I let go of a breath I didn't know I was holding. "Yes," I say.

THIRTY-THREE PENNY WEATHERFORD

I open my eyes and look at the man standing across from me in our cold, dark basement. We're surrounded by boxes of birth certificates, Sunday school drawings, and report cards. Medical records and holiday decorations. The history of our family.

"Richard, I need you to . . ." I have to stop and steady myself before I can continue. He just stares at me. "I need you to tell me everything that happened today. Tell me everything you left out. Who you saw, and when and where you saw them, and what you said to them."

I hear the words come out of my mouth, but my voice sounds hollow and disconnected from my body. My vision drifts to some middle distance between us. I should call the police. But if I do that, Richard will go to prison, and I'll be left with no money, no house, no friends. Nothing but five damaged children and all these boxes. He's brought disaster to our door, but I'm the one who has to open the door and let it in. And I can't do that. God told Abraham to sacrifice his son Isaac on an altar in order to prove his righteousness. Abraham was ready to do it. But I'm not. I've reached the limit of my righteousness. I would rather lose my soul than sacrifice my children.

"We need to go over all of it," I say, "in case you've missed something."

Something like a smile of relief crosses Richard's face. I shake my head.

"No," I say quietly. "Don't smile. Please don't smile. We need to figure out how to best handle this, Richard. We need to do it now, because at any minute the phone's going to ring and it's going to be somebody calling to tell us the news. And that's when we'll have to start living this whole new pack of lies you've made up. If we could die for this without hurting the children, I'd choose that. But we can't. You've taken them hostage.

"So, we need to go over this again, now, while we still have time, so we can figure out what we're going to do. But don't smile like any part of this makes you happy."

"Nothing about this makes me happy," he says. "I'm just exhausted. And knowing you're with me, I guess I'm just . . . I'm relieved."

I have to shut my eyes again. "God forgive us."

The first call comes after we've gone up to bed. Though neither of us can sleep, we want to appear as normal as possible in case one of the kids wakes up. I've changed into my sleepwear—an old VBS T-shirt and some plaid cotton drawstring pants—and he's lying there in boxers and a white T-shirt. Neither of us has spoken in an hour when his cell phone rattles the bedside table.

He sits up and looks at it. "It's Bobby Collins," he tells me, the phone still vibrating in his hand.

Bobby Collins is a deputy at the sheriff's office. He attends our church with his wife, Jonell. Jonell's pregnant with their first child, a girl.

"Remember that he woke you up," I tell Richard. "And put him on speaker."

Richard nods. "Hello," he says.

"Hey, Brother Weatherford," the voice says from the phone, "this is Bobby Collins. I'm sorry to disturb you this early in the morning."

"It's all right, Bobby. Is everything okay?"

"No, sir, I'm afraid not. There's been a terrible accident. You know Gary Doane, goes to our church?"

"Gary, yes."

"Well, I'm afraid it involves him and his girlfriend, Sarabeth. You know, Sarabeth Simmons?"

"Sarabeth . . . Yeah I think so. I'm not sure I ever met her, though."

"Well, they went off that little side road that runs down by the Little Red River. They were both killed."

"Oh, my Lord," Richard says.

"Well, sir, the reason I'm calling you is because Gary's dad is up here. He's a mess. I wonder if you wouldn't mind coming down and maybe taking him home. Reason I ask, the sheriff would like to clear the scene. And Vaughn's in a pretty agitated state. If he becomes too much of a disturbance, I'm afraid the sheriff's gonna order us to restrain him. I'd rather not have to do that . . ."

"Of course, I'll be right down. Be there in a few minutes."

I stand up and begin dressing before Richard hangs up the phone.

"There's no reason for you to come," he says. "I can—"

"I'm coming," I say. "Hurry and get dressed."

When I've tied my tennis shoes, I ease open our bedroom door and creep down the hall to Matthew's room. He's still asleep. I walk over and shake his arm. "Matt, honey, wake up. Wake up."

He wipes his eyes with the back of his hand and asks, "Mom? What's wrong?"

"There's been an accident involving some people at the church. Your dad and I need to go see if we can help."

His hair is splayed on one side, his voice drowsy. "Should I go?"

"No, you stay here. I don't know how long we'll be. What I need you to do is make sure everyone is ready for church as usual. I'll call with any information."

He's blinking. "What time is it?"

"Almost five."

"Who was it?"

"What?"

"In the accident, from our church, who was it?"

"Gary Doane."

My husband and I ride in silence to the scene of his crime. The night is still clinging to the sky, and the familiar sights of our neighborhood seem strange, the houses lined up as orderly as tombstones. As we wind our way down the hill toward the bridge, I can see unnaturally bright blue police lights flickering along the river. Then I notice that there's also the red light of an ambulance.

"Why is there an ambulance?" I ask. My stomach is sick.

"Normal procedure," he says.

"If someone is alive down there . . ."

"No one is alive down there. I can assure you of that."

What a thing to say. This is my husband. This is my life now.

We cross the bridge and turn onto the small dirt road leading down to the river. A patrol car is parked in the middle of the road to bar entry, and a young officer I don't know flags us down.

When Richard lowers his window, the officer says, "Can't come down here, sir. Got a bad accident."

"I'm Richard Weatherford," my husband says. "Bobby Collins called me and asked us to help with Vaughn Doane. I'm the preacher up at First Baptist."

The officer says, "He left."

"Vaughn?"

"Yessir, left about two minutes ago. Maybe even just one minute. You just missed him."

"Oh."

"Hold on a sec." The officer leans into the microphone clipped to his shirt. "Come again?" he says. I don't hear what the person on the other end says, but the officer replies, "It's Richard Weatherford, preacher at the Baptist church. Says Bobby called him . . . Yessir. Roger that." He turns to us. "Could you hang here a second, Brother Weatherford? The sheriff is headed this way, and I think he'd like to stop and have a word with you."

"Sure."

The officer heads back to his car. Neither Richard nor I say a thing, but I can hear my own breath. I hear him swallow.

The sheriff drives up the hill. He parks next to the young officer, gets out of the car, gives some instructions, and then strolls up to us.

I've never had a conversation with Bud Ison, though I've seen him around. He's tall and muscular and carries himself like a military man. I know his wife, Cynthia, from the PTA. They're Methodists and have three sons.

"Brother Weatherford," the sheriff says. He nods at me. "Ma'am. Thank you both for getting out of bed at this hour of the morning. I'm afraid Mr. Doane was in a state of agitation. Understandable, of course, but I had to ask him to go on home. I had Bobby follow him, make sure he gets there okay. I'm sorry y'all had to come down for nothing."

"Not a problem," Richard says. "I'm just sorry I couldn't help."

"Do you know what happened?" I ask.

"Well, it's Gary and Sarabeth. Sarabeth Simmons. They're both dead."

"Oh, my Lord," I say. "Any idea what happened?"

"Well, I shouldn't really discuss it, ma'am. But I got some questions. Let's put it that way. I know a couple of guys I want to talk to."

"You think someone—"

Richard gently reaches for my hand to shut me up, but the sheriff doesn't notice because someone is shouting over his microphone. "Holy shit, sir! We got another body down here."

"Come again?"

"Yessir, we got a body. This one's in the water, and you ain't gonna believe who it is."

The sheriff's face changes color. He nods at us and hurries back to his car without a word. We watch him race back down the hill, dust billowing in his wake.

⁂

We drive back in silence. Vaughn Doane is probably home by now. He's trying to tell Jill what happened. Trying to tell Jill that her son is dead.

"Pull over," I say.

"What?"

"Pull over!"

Richard swerves into a grassy ditch, and I almost fall out of the car. I think I'll vomit, but I don't. I'm bent over, staring at the dew glistening on the ditch's thick weeds and wild flowers.

When I know I'll be okay, I walk back to the car and get in.

Richard doesn't speak as we drive back toward our home.

I tell him, "You need to call Vaughn as soon as we get home and see what he knows."

"Don't you think I should wait and see what they come up with first?"

"No. You should call to let him know that you heard about Gary. You don't want him to find out later that you were at the scene this morning and didn't think to call. Under any normal circumstance, you'd call." I turn to him. "You're afraid of talking to him. You feel guilty because you killed his son. But it's too late for that. If you were going to feel bad, you should have felt bad about sleeping with a boy as old as Matthew."

I can feel my hate for him growing with every word. So can he. His face hardens.

"You'll call Vaughn," I say. "Later today, or maybe tomorrow, I'll call Jill. When the time's right, we'll go to their home and sit and pray with them." I look out the window at the tombstones going by as the sky starts to whiten with the first sunlight. "We need to make ourselves indispensable to the Doanes."

He nods. "I'll call Vaughn when we get home."

"Good."

He looks over at me for a moment. "What are you going to do now?"

I look down at my bare fingernails. "What do you think? I'm going to get ready for church."

I shower, letting the water lap over my body in cold gushes. I'm so tight I could snap. I wish I had alcohol or pills. I wish I could pray. But I have none of that to call on. When I finally shut off the water, my skin, white and covered in drops, feels as tight as my insides.

I step out of the shower, wrapping a towel around my chest.

Richard taps on the door.

"Come in," I say.

He pokes his head in. "I just wanted to tell you I called Vaughn."

"I said to come in. Come all the way into the bathroom and shut the door behind you."

He steps in and closes the door. Our images in the steamed bathroom mirror are blurred, unrecognizable.

"I called Vaughn," he says.

"And?"

"He couldn't really talk. He was crying."

"He's crying because his son is dead."

Richard looks down. "Yes."

"What did you expect?"

"Expect? Nothing. I knew he'd be upset. I just thought I should tell you."

"Well, you told me."

"Yes. Okay. I'll go and let you get ready . . ."

He reaches for the door.

"Richard."

He stops and turns back to me.

I look at him, standing there in his jeans and his sneakers and the old T-shirt. Hatred warms my skin.

"Get on your knees."

"What are you talking about?"

"Now. Get on your knees."

Instead, he frowns and reaches for the door, turning the knob and opening it an inch before I kick it shut.

"What are you doing?" he says.

"Get on your knees, Richard."

"I—"

"There's nothing you need to say. Get down on your knees, Richard. Do it now. Don't make me tell you again."

He looks at me, his mouth open, searching for words. He tries to summon his incredulous smile, that fake thing he uses as a cudgel, but he can't quite make it happen. He can't call on any of his old tricks, can't just be the same Richard he's always been. He can't just dismiss me, not anymore.

Watching him finally lower himself to his knees makes me wet.

"On your hands."

"Penny . . ."

I lean over and grab his throat. His neck is bigger than my hand, but I can grasp his throat, can feel its ridged cartilage between my fingers. "Get down on your hands."

He lowers himself to his hands.

I loosen the damp towel, and it flops onto the vanity, hanging off an open drawer and slapping the floor. I spread my legs and grab Richard's head, balling up his hair in my fist, and push his face between my thighs. Water drips from my hair, mixed now with sweat, and drops onto his forehead, into his eyes.

"Lick."

PART THREE SUNDAY MORNING

ONE YEAR LATER

THIRTY-FOUR RICHARD WEATHERFORD

"Jesus Christ died on Good Friday and rose again on Easter Sunday, but on Black Saturday he lay dead in his tomb as his followers trembled alone in their doubt. That was over two thousand years ago, but this morning I know that some of you are still trembling."

I look out over the congregation. The pews are packed this morning, even for an Easter service, reflecting the fact that attendance has been climbing all year. Most of the old familiar faces are here, joined by new members and the usual mixture of visiting family and holiday-only Christians. Pastel splashes of yellow, pink, and purple enliven the usual clothing choices. More people dress up for Easter than for our usual services.

"God does not want us to be alone. God does not want us to stumble in darkness. God does not want us to shiver in the cold. God will be your constant companion, your light in the darkness, your warm shelter against the freezing wind."

I move to the edge of the stage.

"I want to thank all the performers today for their skill and dedication in bringing us the music and drama of the Easter program. It was wonderful. But before we go off to enjoy the rest of this special day, I need to tell you the truth."

The members of my family occupy their usual places on the third row. Penny with her arm around Johnny. Matthew next to his fiancée, Sydnie. Mark sitting with Ruth.

Only Mary is missing, the first time one of our children has not been with us at Easter. She says it means nothing. She has too much schoolwork, she says. I suspect otherwise, and I know that Penny harbors her own theories about our eldest daughter.

But the others are in their proper place, the place they have been for so long. Watching me, listening to me, loving me. Unlike the children, unlike anyone here, Penny watches me with a cool expression on her face, the distance between us the distance between critic and performer. Her judgment is cold, precise, and silent.

"Yes, I need to tell you the truth," I say again. "And the truth is that life is loss."

The congregation squirms at this notion. *Life is loss*, after all, is not a comforting thought, and this uncomfortable thought is both unexpected and unwelcome, a sudden shadow at the end of our sunny Easter service.

"Life is loss," I say, "and the truth is that we will lose everyone in this life. At the end of every relationship—whether it begins with a boy asking a girl out on a date, or it begins with a mother holding her baby for the first time—at the end of every relationship is a grave. We want so desperately for things to be permanent, but they are not.

"We tremble at this thought. This thought, this absolute certainly that we will lose everyone . . . it's simply too large, too overwhelming for us to keep in our minds for more than a few moments. But we know it's true, and this knowledge haunts us. We will die, and when we do, our body will descend into the same dark grave that is the destiny of every man, woman, and child.

"Death is the meaning of life, my friends. Why are the symbols of our faith the cross and the tomb? It's to remind us that the meaning of life is death. We will lose everyone we love. If we don't lose them first, they will lose us.

"Some well-meaning souls say, 'Well, the important thing is what you leave behind.' It's a nice thought. But the hard truth is that the world won't miss a beat when any of us goes. The day I die, the traffic lights will keep changing from red to green, and Burger King will keep selling hamburgers, and the world will just go on about its business. 'Well, what about your beloved children? They'll miss you.' And of course, that's true. But one day they'll be gone, and then one day their children will be gone, and then no one in this world will have a living memory of me. It will be for me as it will be for everyone in this room; it will be as if I had never existed at all."

The church is silent. They are waiting. I've told them that the beginning of knowledge is the truth that life itself is fragile and finite. But they're waiting for the lie.

So I give it to them. I soothe them with a beautiful and elaborate untruth: I tell them that death is not really death. I turn and face the cross, and I tell them that Christ descended into the grave and he rose again, bringing us the gift of eternal life. I tell them that there is no death beyond the veil for those who accept this gift.

I turn back to them. Most of them believe me. Most of them have never given the question of life and death serious thought. Most of them were told as children that the death of Jesus somehow means that they themselves will never really die, and they have believed it ever since. Although the exact mechanics of this theology are as uninteresting to them as the exact mechanics of their cell phone, their theology, like their phone, does what it is supposed to do. That's all they need to know.

"Remember what Paul wrote to the Corinthians," I tell them. "'Death, where is thy sting? Death, where is thy victory?'"

I tell them that death is dead. I tell them that Jesus killed it. I tell them that they can live forever in heaven.

Most of them believe me. They want to believe me.

Among the crowd, however, disbelief is written on the features of two faces. These people cannot believe me, yet they are both here for the same reason.

Carmen Fuller has never attended this church as far as I can remember. Perhaps she came by once, years ago, to pick up her daughter, Sarabeth, from the youth group. If so, I missed her. I know her only as a face around town. I pass her in the aisles at Walmart. I gas up next to her at Exxon. She is a thin, haggard woman with disappointed eyes and a smoker's cough.

She sits near the back, staring into space. She came to church today hoping, I am sure, to find some peace of mind on the anniversary of her daughter's death.

Just a few rows in front of her sits Vaughn Doane. They do not acknowledge each other. He is alone today, as alone as Carmen. His wife, Jill, refuses to come to church. The death of her son a year ago shattered whatever faith she once had. Vaughn has told me that she's angry at God, though I suspect it's truer to say that she's angry that her husband keeps on believing in a God who has failed them so utterly.

Vaughn must believe, though. He is one of those people, bless him. He must believe or surrender to the deep. His faith is the only buoy keeping him afloat in his despair.

I ask for anyone to come forward if they would like to accept Christ as their savior or to rededicate their lives to Christ.

There are no new converts or rededications, which is a bit of a disappointment because I liked my sermon, but I am not terribly surprised. People rarely get saved at an Easter service. Most people just want to go home and eat.

But when I ask if anyone would like to pray with me for any other reason, Vaughn steps out from his pew, his suit wrinkled, his tie askew. He wants to pray with me. I knew he would. Most of the people in attendance today already know why he's walking up this carpeted aisle with tears glistening in his eyes. They lean forward in their seats.

His son died one year ago. In the early hours of Easter morning, Vaughn and Jill were awakened when their son left their car in the driveway and then rode away with his girlfriend, Sarabeth. Over the next hour, Vaughn and Jill both tried calling Gary several times. After getting no response, they called the county sheriff's office. The police didn't regard this as an emergency but promised to be on the lookout for Gary and told Vaughn to stay home.

Vaughn didn't listen. He got in his car and headed for the center of downtown. As he neared the bridge, the bridge not far from this church where I am now holding out my arms to receive Vaughn, he saw flashing blue lights scattered along the Little Red River.

"I just knew," he told me later. "When I saw those lights, I just knew that he was dead."

Of course, that morning, as the terrible reality made itself clear, he couldn't know how or why his son had died. The police would piece together the story over the coming days: how Gary Doane, Sarabeth Simmons, and Brian Harten had conspired to steal from Tommy Weller, how Harten had set fire to Tommy's statue while Sarabeth stayed in the front of the bar and Gary snuck into the back. Tommy Weller, having discovered what happened, first confronted Harten, and then forced Harten to help him find the young lovers. During the confrontation, however, Harten shot Weller and bludgeoned him to death with his baseball bat. When the trio were disposing of the body at the bridge, apparently Gary turned on Harten with the bat, fractured his skull, and pushed him into the river to drown. Then, apparently panicking, Gary and Sarabeth drove down to the river, perhaps to pull one or both of the bodies out of the water. In her panicked state, Sarabeth ran off the road, killing both of them.

Evidence came together quickly and clearly. Police questioned Harten's ex-wife, who confirmed that he'd borrowed her car to go see Weller, only to return the vehicle several hours late reeking of gasoline. Two waitresses at the bar witnessed an argument between Harten and Weller over money. Police spoke to a station owner in Birdtown who remembered selling Harten a curiously small amount of gas just before the fire. Patrons at the bar placed Sarabeth there when the statue burned down, and they reported that she left before law enforcement arrived to investigate. Not long after the fire, the sheriff himself pulled over Weller for speeding and discovered that Harten was his passenger. Weller admitted to the sheriff that he had already been in a physical altercation with Gary and Sarabeth just after the fire, and text messages between Weller and Sarabeth confirm that he was trying to recover his money from the couple. Investigators found drops of Harten's blood on the railing of the bridge. Although the current carried Weller's corpse more than a mile down the river, Harten drowned just below the bridge and his body swept ashore shortly thereafter, allowing the forensics team to uncover traces of gunpowder and Weller's blood beneath his fingernails. Both Weller's gun and the missing money, nearly twenty thousand dollars in small bills, some of it containing blood residue from both Weller and Harten, were found on the floorboard of Sarabeth's crushed car.

Most of the people in church today know some, if not all, of these details. Most of us knew one or more of the deceased, and the Doanes have been members of this congregation for years. I was able to help police piece together the frame of mind of both Gary and Brian, since I spoke to both of them on the day they died. I was saddened to confirm for investigators that Gary was indeed a depressed young man involved with a girl of low character, and that Brian, realizing that his attempt to turn the county wet was doomed, seemed desperate and incoherent.

People still ask me about these terrible events all the time, and I tell them what Paul told the church in Rome: "The wages of sin is death, but the free gift of God is life everlasting."

When Vaughn, poor man, reaches me, he weeps in my arms. The church knows why. No one fidgets, not even the children, and this Easter crowd is no longer hungry for lunch, no longer restless to get back to their televisions. Nothing on television can compete with the live theater of a church service operating at its highest level. Deep down, though many of them don't know it, this is why they come to church in the first place. It isn't for the neutered music or the creaky theology. It is for the possibility of seeing genuine human frailty laid bare, the same frailty that all the food, beer, and football cannot help them deny. They know what this grief is. We all know what this grief is.

Vaughn's weeping, his public confession of powerlessness, is the only redemption available to any of us. No invisible deity worries over us; no ancient text can save us. This man has been broken by life's cruelty, brutalized by the universe's utter indifference to his suffering. He needs something to hold on to, needs someone to hold him up so that he does not disappear into the darkest regions of human despair.

He needs me.

ACKNOWLEDGMENTS

First, I need to thank my agent Nat Sobel. Your insights into this book and your efforts on its behalf were invaluable. Sincere thanks to the whole team at Sobel Weber Associates.

Thanks to my wonderful editor Katie McGuire and the team at Pegasus Books, especially Andrea Monagle, Dan O'Connor, and Sabrina Plomitallo-González.

To the great Oliver Gallmeister, merci beaucoup. And thanks to everyone at éditions Gallmeister, particularly my brilliant translator Sophie Aslanides.

To Heather Brown, Lindsey Muller, Jay Varner, Chris McSween, and Patrick Culliton, my deep gratitude for your love and friendship.

To all the Hinksons, my continuing thanks for your love and forbearance.

And for Anne-Sophie Rouveloux, preuve d'amour. Je t'aime, ma cacahuète.

21982319235887